The Everyman

P. G. WODEHOUSE

The Old Reliable

EVERYMAN

Published by Everyman's Library
Northburgh House
10 Northburgh Street
London EC1V 0AT

First published by Herbert Jenkins, 1951
Published by Everyman's Library, 2011

Typography by Peter B. Willberg

ISBN 978-1-84159-178-0

A CIP catalogue record for this book is available from the British Library

Distributed by Random House (UK) Ltd.,
20 Vauxhall Bridge Road, London SW1V 2SA

Typeset by AccComputing, North Barrow, Somerset
Printed and bound in Germany
by GGP Media GmbH, Pössneck

The Old Reliable

The sunshine which is such an agreeable feature of life in and around Hollywood, when the weather is not unusual, blazed down from a sky of turquoise blue on the spacious grounds of what, though that tempestuous Mexican star had ceased for nearly a year to be its owner and it was now the property of Mrs Adela Shannon Cork, was still known locally as the Carmen Flores place. The month was May, the hour noon.

The Carmen Flores place stood high up in the mountains at the point where Alamo Drive peters out into a mere dirt track fringed with cactus and rattlesnakes, and the rays of the sun illumined its swimming pool, its rose garden, its orange trees, its lemon trees, its jacaranda trees and its stone-flagged terrace. Sunshine, one might say, was everywhere, excepting only in the heart of the large, stout, elderly gentleman seated on the terrace, who looked like a Roman emperor who had been doing himself too well on starchy foods and forgetting to watch his calories. His name was Smedley Cork, he was the brother of Mrs Adela Cork's late husband, and he was gazing in a sullen, trapped sort of way at an object which had just appeared on the skyline.

This was a butler, an unmistakably English butler, tall, decorous and dignified, who was advancing toward him carrying on a salver a brimming glass that contained a white liquid.

Everything in Mrs Cork's domain spoke eloquently of wealth and luxury, but nothing more eloquently than the presence on the premises of this Phipps. In Beverly Hills, as a general thing, the householder employs a 'couple', who prove totally incompetent and leave the following week, to be succeeded by another couple, equally subhuman. A Filipino butler indicates a certain modest degree of stepping out. An English butler means magnificence. Nobody can go higher than that.

'Your yoghurt, sir,' said Phipps, like a benevolent uncle bestowing a gift on a deserving child.

Lost in daydreams, as he so often was when he sat on the terrace in the sunshine, Smedley had forgotten all about the yoghurt which his sister-in-law compelled him to drink at this time of the day in place of the more conventional cocktail. He sniffed at the glass with a shrinking distaste, and gave it as his opinion that it smelled like a motorman's glove.

The butler's manner, respectful and sympathetic, seemed to suggest that he agreed that there existed certain points of resemblance.

'It is, however, excellent for the health, I believe, sir. Bulgarian peasants drink it in large quantities. It makes them rosy.'

'Well, who wants a rosy Bulgarian peasant?'

'There is that, of course, sir.'

'You find a rosy Bulgarian peasant, you can keep him, see?'

'Thank you very much, sir.'

With a powerful effort Smedley forced himself to swallow a portion of the unpleasant stuff. Coming up for breath, he gave the campus of the University of Southern California at Los Angeles, which lay beneath him in the valley, a nasty look.

'What a life!' he said.

'Yes, sir.'

'It shouldn't happen to a dog.'

'The world is full of sadness, sir,' sighed Phipps.

Smedley resented this remark, helpful though he realized it was intended to be.

'A fat lot you know about sadness,' he said hotly. 'You're a carefree butler. If you don't like it here, you can go elsewhere, see what I mean? I can't, see what I mean? You ever been in prison, Phipps?'

The butler started.

'Sir?'

'No, of course you haven't. Then you wouldn't understand.'

Smedley finished the yoghurt and fell into a moody silence. He was thinking of the will of the late Alfred Cork and feeling how strange and tragic it was that different people should so differently interpret a testator's wishes.

That clause which Al had inserted, enjoining his widow to 'support' his brother Smedley. There you had a typical instance of the way confusion and misunderstanding could arise. As Smedley saw it, when you instruct a woman to support some-body, you mean that you expect her to set him up in an apartment on Park Avenue with an income sufficient to enable him to maintain the same and run a car and belong to a few good clubs and take that annual trip to Paris or Rome or Bermuda or wher-ever it may be, and so on and so forth. Adela, more frugal in her views, had understood the bequest as limiting her obligations to the provision of a bed, three meals a day and the run of the house, and it was on these lines that her brother-in-law's life had pro-ceeded. The unfortunate man ate well and slept well and had all the yoghurt he wanted, but apart from that his lot these last few years had been substantially that of a convict serving a sentence in a penitentiary.

He came out of his reverie with a grunt. There swept over him an urge to take this kindly butler into his confidence, concealing nothing.

'You know what I am, Phipps?'

'Sir?'

'I'm a bird in a gilded cage.'

'Indeed, sir?'

'I'm a worm.'

'You are getting me confused, sir. I understood you to say that you were a bird.'

'A worm, too. A miserable, downtrodden Hey-you of a worm on whose horizon there is no ray of light. What are those things they have in Mexico?'

'Tamales, sir?'

'Peons. I'm just a peon. Ordered hither, ordered thither, ground beneath the iron heel, treated like a dog. And the bitter part is that I used to have a lot of money once. A pot of money. All gone now.'

'Indeed, sir?'

'Yes, all gone. Ran through it. Wasted my substance. What a lesson this should be to all of us, Phipps, not to waste our substance.'

'Yes, sir.'

'A fool's game, wasting your substance. No percentage in it. If you don't have substance, where are you?'

'Precisely, sir.'

'Precisely, sir, is right. Can you lend me a hundred dollars?'

'No, sir.'

Smedley had not really hoped. But the sudden desire which had come to him for just one night out in the brighter spots of Los Angeles and district had been so imperious that he had thought it worth while to bring the subject up. Butlers, he knew, salted their cash away, and he was a great believer in sharing the wealth.

'How about fifty?'

'No, sir.'

'I'd settle for fifty,' said Smedley, who was not an unreasonable man, and knew that there are times when one must make concessions.

'No, sir.'

Smedley gave it up. He saw too late that it had been a mistake to dish out that stuff about wasting one's substance. Simply putting ideas into the fellow's head. He sat for a moment scowling darkly, then suddenly brightened. He had just remembered that good old Bill had arrived in this ghastly house yesterday. It altered the whole aspect of affairs. How he had come to overlook such a promising source of revenue, he could not imagine. Wilhelmina ('Bill') Shannon was Adela's sister and consequently his sister-in-law by marriage, and if there was anything in the theory that blood is thicker than water, she should surely be good for a trifling sum like a hundred dollars. Besides, he had known dear old Bill since he was so high.

'Where's Miss Shannon?' he asked.

'In the Garden Room, sir. I believe she is working on Mrs Cork's *Memoirs*.'

'Right. Thank you, Phipps.'

'Thank you, sir.'

The butler made a stately exit, and Smedley, feeling a little drowsy, decided that later on would be time enough for going into committee of supply with Bill. He closed his eyes, and presently soft snores began to blend with the humming of the local insects and the rustle of the leaves in the tree above him.

The good man taking his rest.

* * *

Phipps, back in his pantry, was restoring his tissues with an iced lemonade. He frowned as he sipped the wholesome beverage, and his air was tense and preoccupied. The household cat brushed itself insinuatingly against his legs, but he remained unresponsive to its overtures. There is a time for tickling cats under the ear and a time for not tickling cats under the ear.

When Smedley Cork, in their conversation on the terrace, had described James Phipps as carefree, he had been misled, as casual observers are so apt to be misled, by the fact that butlers, like oysters, wear the mask and do not show their emotions. Carefree was the last adjective that could fittingly have been applied to the sombre man as he sat there in his pantry, brooding, brooding. If he had had his elbow on his knee and his chin in his hand, he might have been posing for Rodin's *Penseur*.

It was on Wilhelmina Shannon that he was brooding, as he had been doing almost incessantly since he had admitted her at the front door on the previous afternoon. He was cursing the malignant fate that had brought her to this house and asking himself for the hundredth time what, now that she was here, the harvest would be. It was the old, old story. The woman knew too much. His future hung on her silence, and the question that was agitating James Phipps was, were women ever silent? True, the balloon had not yet gone up, which argued his secret was still unrevealed, but could this happy state of things persist?

A bell rang, and he saw that it was that of the Garden Room. Duty, stern daughter of the voice of God, said Phipps to himself, or words to that effect, and left his lemonade and made his way thither.

The Garden Room of the Carmen Flores place was the one next to the library and immediately below the projection room, a cheerful apartment with a large desk beside the french windows that looked on the swimming pool. It caught the morning sun, and for those who liked it there was a fine view of the oil wells over by the coast. Bill Shannon, seated at the desk with the tube of a dictaphone in her hand, was too busy at the moment to look at oil wells. As Phipps had indicated, she was forcing herself to concentrate on the exacting task of composing her sister Adela's *Memoirs*.

Bill Shannon was a breezy, hearty, genial woman in the early forties, built on generous lines and clad in comfortable slacks. Rugged was a term that might have been applied to her face with its high cheekbones and masterful chin, but large, humorous eyes of a bright blue relieved this ruggedness and rendered her, if not spectacularly beautiful like her sister Adela, definitely attractive. Her disposition was amiable, and as a mixer she was second to none. Everybody liked Bill Shannon, even in Hollywood, where nobody likes anybody.

She raised the mouthpiece of the dictaphone and began to speak into it, if 'speak' is not too weak a word. Her voice was a very powerful contralto, and Joe Davenport, a young friend of hers with whom she had worked on the Superba-Llewellyn lot, had sometimes complained that she was apt to use it as if she were chatting with a slightly deaf acquaintance in China. It was Joe's opinion that, if all other sources of income failed, she could always make a good living calling hogs in one of the Western states.

'Hollywood!' boomed Bill. 'How shall I describe the emotions which filled me on that morning when I first came to Hollywood, an eager wide-eyed girl of sixteen . . . Liar! You were nearly twenty . . . So young, so unsophisticated. Just a—'

The door opened. Phipps appeared. Bill held up a hand.

'—timid little tot,' she concluded. 'Yes, Phipps?'

'You rang, madam.'

Bill nodded.

'Oh, yes. I want to confer with you in your executive capacity, Phipps. What with one thing and another, it has suddenly been borne in upon me that if I don't get a quick restorative, I shall expire. Have you ever written the *Memoirs* of a silent film star?'

'No, madam.'

'It is a task that taxes the physique to the uttermost.'

'No doubt, madam.'

'So will you bring me a fairly strong whisky and soda?'

'Yes, madam.'

'You really ought to go around with a keg of brandy attached to your neck, like Saint Bernard dogs in the Alps. No delay that way. No time lag.'

'No, madam.'

Bill, who had been sitting with her feet on the desk, put them down. She swivelled around in her chair and fixed her bright blue gaze on the butler. This was the first opportunity she had had since her arrival of a private and undisturbed talk with him, and it seemed to her that they had much to discuss.

'You're very curt and monosyllabic, Brother Phipps. Your manner is aloof. It is as though you felt in my presence a certain constraint and embarrassment. Do you?'

'Yes, madam.'

'I'm not surprised. It's your conscience that makes you feel that way. I know your secret, Phipps.'

'Yes, madam.'

'I recognized you the moment I saw you, of course. Yours is a face that impresses itself on the mental retina. And now I suppose you're wondering what I propose to do about it?'

'Yes, madam.'

Bill smiled. She had a delightful smile which lit up her whole face as if some inner lamp had been switched on, and Phipps, seeing it, was conscious for the first time since three o'clock on the previous afternoon of a lessening of the weight that pressed upon his heavy soul.

'Not a thing,' said Bill. 'My lips are sealed. The awful truth is safe with me. So be of good cheer, Phipps, and unleash that merry laugh of yours, of which I hear such good reports.'

Phipps did not laugh, for laughter is not permitted to English butlers by the rules of their Guild, but he allowed his lips to twitch slightly and gazed at this noble woman with something approaching adoration, an emotion which he had never expected to feel for a member of the jury which three years before had sent him up the river for what the Press of New York was unanimous in describing as a well-earned sentence. It was a moment or two before he was able to clothe his feelings in words.

'I am sure I am extremely grateful to you for your kindness, madam. You relieve my apprehensions. I am most anxious not to lose my position here.'

'Why? You could get a job anywhere. Walk into any house in Beverly Hills, and they'll lay down the red carpet for you.'

'Yes, madam, but there are reasons why I do not wish to leave Mrs Cork's service.'

'What reasons?'

'Personal reasons, madam.'

'I see. Well, I won't give you away.'

'Thank you very much, madam.'

'I am only sorry that I have occasioned you alarm and despondency. It must have given you a nasty jolt when you opened that front door yesterday and I walked in.'

'Yes, madam.'

'You must have felt like Macbeth seeing Banquo's ghost.'

'My emotions were somewhat similar, madam.'

Bill lit a cigarette.

'Rather odd that you should have remembered me. But I suppose, in the position you were in when we met, you've nothing much to do except study the faces of the jury.'

'No, madam. It passes the time.'

'Too bad we had to send you up.'

'Yes, madam.'

'But we couldn't go against the evidence.'

'No, madam. But might I beg you to lower your voice, madam. Walls have ears.'

'Walls have what?'

'Ears, madam.'

'Oh, ears! That's right. They have, haven't they? What was it like in Sing-Sing?' whispered Bill.

'Not very agreeable, madam,' whispered Phipps.

'No, I imagine not,' whispered Bill. 'Oh, hello, Smedley.'

Smedley Cork, his siesta concluded, had appeared in the french window.

Phipps left the room, followed by the austere and disapproving look which impecunious elderly gentlemen give a butler who has refused to lend them a hundred dollars, and Smedley took a seat on the sofa.

'I want to talk to you, Bill,' he said.

'And so you shall, pal. What's on your mind? My God, Smedley,' said Bill with the candour of a friend of twenty-five years' standing, 'you've aged terribly since I saw you last. I was shocked when I got here and observed what a museum piece you had become. Your hair's as grey as a badger.'

'I'm thinking of having it touched up.'

'It won't do any good. There's only one real cure for grey hair. It was invented by a Frenchman. He called it the guillotine. I suppose it's living with Adela that's done it. I can't imagine anything more calculated to produce silver threads among the gold than constant association with that sister of mine.'

Her words were music to Smedley's ears. He basked in her sympathy. Good old Bill, he told himself, had always been sympathetic. So much so that once or twice only that instinct for self-preservation which saves Nature's bachelors in their hour of need had prevented him from asking her to marry him. Occasionally, in black moods, he regretted this. Then the black mood would pass. The mere thought of being married appalled Smedley.

'It's a dog's life,' he agreed. 'She oppresses me, Bill. I'd be better off in Alcatraz. At least I wouldn't have to drink yoghurt there.'

'Does Adela make you drink yoghurt?'

'Every day.'

'Inhuman. Of course, it's good for you.'

Smedley held up a protesting hand.

'Just as a favour,' he begged, 'don't mention those Bulgarian peasants.'

'Which Bulgarian peasants would those be?'

'The ones it makes rosy.'

'Does yoghurt make Bulgarian peasants rosy?'

'So Phipps says.'

A deep chuckle escaped Bill Shannon.

'Phipps! If my lips weren't sealed, I could tell you something about Phipps. Ever hear of still waters?'

'What about them?'

'They run deep. That's Phipps. What a man! I suppose you

look on him as just the ordinary sort of stage butler. Let me tell you that Brother Phipps has quite another side to him. However, as I say, my lips are sealed, so it's no use you trying to institute a probe.'

Smedley was perplexed.

'How do you know anything about Phipps? You only got here yesterday. Had you met him before?'

'I had, and in curious circumstances. But don't ask questions.'

'I don't want to ask questions. I'm not interested in Phipps. I'm off Phipps for life. He has hurt and disappointed me.'

'You don't say? What was the trouble?'

'I asked him for a small loan just now, and would you believe it,' said Smedley, with honest indignation, 'he refused. Turned me down flat. "No, sir," he said. And the fellow's probably rolling in money. Thank heaven for people like you, Bill. You wouldn't do that sort of thing. You're big-hearted. You're a pal, as true as steel. Good old Bill! Dear old Bill! Could you lend me a hundred dollars, Bill?'

Bill blinked. Well though she knew Smedley, she had not seen it coming.

'A hundred dollars?'

'I need it sorely.'

'Are you planning to go on a toot?'

'Yes,' cried Smedley passionately. 'I am. The toot of a lifetime, if I can raise the necessary funds. Do you realize that I haven't had a night out for five years? It's as much as I can do to get the price of a packet of cigarettes out of Adela. I'm just a worm in a gilded cage. So you will let me have that hundred, won't you, Bill?'

A look of gentle pity had come into Bill's blue eyes. Her heart ached for this tortured soul.

'If I had a hundred dollars, my poor broken blossom,' she said, 'I'd give it you like a shot. I think a toot is just what you need, to bring the roses back to your cheeks. But I'm as fiscally crippled as you are. You don't suppose I'd be here, ghostwriting the story of Adela's unspeakably dull life, if I had cash in the bank, do you?' She patted his shoulder commiseratingly. 'I'm afraid I've spoiled your day. I'm sorry. What a lot of succotash people talk about poverty making you spiritual,' she proceeded, in moralizing vein. 'All it's ever done to me is make me envious of the lucky stiffs who've got the stuff, like that boy who used to work with me on the Superba-Llewellyn lot. Did I tell you about him? Got fired, went back to New York, and the first thing you know he wins one of those big radio jackpots. Twenty-four thousand bucks, they said it was in the papers. Would that sort of thing ever happen to me? No, sir, not in a million years.'

'Nor to me. But—'

Smedley paused. He looked cautiously over his shoulder. He looked cautiously over his other shoulder. Then he turned and looked cautiously behind him.

'But what?' said Bill, mystified by these manœuvres.

Smedley lowered his voice to a conspiratorial whisper.

'I'll tell you something, Bill.'

'Well, tell it louder. I can't hear a word.'

'It isn't a thing you can shout from the house tops,' said Smedley, still conspiratorial. 'If Adela got to hear of it, phut would go any chance I have of becoming a rich man.'

'You haven't any chance of becoming a rich man.'

'That,' said Smedley, 'is where you're wrong. I have, if things pan out as I hope they will. Bill, do you know who this house used to belong to?'

'Of course I do. It's a landmark. Carmen Flores.'

'Exactly. Adela bought it furnished from her estate. All her belongings are still here, just as they were the day when she was killed in that plane crash. Get that. All her belongings.'

'So what?'

Smedley glanced over his shoulder again. He lowered his voice again. If in repose he had looked like a Roman Emperor, he now looked like a Roman Emperor talking over a prospective murder with his second vice-president in charge of assassinations.

'Carmen Flores kept a diary.'

'Did she?'

'So everyone says. I'm looking for it.'

'Why, are you thinking of writing her biography?'

'And if I find it, I'll be on velvet. Think, Bill. Reflect. You know what she was like. Always having violent affairs with all sorts of important characters – stars, studio bosses and what have you – and no doubt writing it up in her tablets at her leisure. Why, finding that diary would be like finding a deposit of uranium.'

'You mean that some of the men up top would pay highly to suppress the little brochure?'

'Practically all the men up top.'

Bill regarded him tenderly. She had always been devoted to Smedley, though far from blind to the numerous defects in his spiritual make-up. If there was a lazier man in the world than Smedley Cork, she had never met him. If there was one more refreshingly free from principles of any kind, she had still to make his acquaintance. He was selfish, idle and practically everything else that he ought not to be. Nevertheless, she loved him. She had loved him twenty years ago when he was a young man with money and one chin. She loved him now, when he was a portly senior with no money and two chins. Women do these things.

'In other words,' she said, 'you are hoping to cash in on a little blackmail.'

'It isn't blackmail,' said Smedley indignantly. 'It's a perfectly ordinary, straightforward business transaction. They want the diary, I have it.'

'But you haven't.'

'Well, if I had, I mean.'

Bill laughed indulgently. The proposition, as outlined, seemed to her pure Smedley. It did not weaken in the slightest her love for him. If someone had come to her and said: 'Wilhelmina Shannon, you are wasting your affection on a totally unworthy object,' she would have replied, 'Yessir. And I like it.' She was a one-man woman.

'You'll never make your fortune, Smedley, honestly or dishonestly. Now, I shall – I don't know how, but somehow. And when I do, I'm going to marry you.'

Smedley quivered.

'Don't say such things, even in fun.'

'I'm not being funny. I've given the matter a good deal of thought these last twenty years, and when I got here and saw what was left of you after living with Adela all this time, I made up my mind there was only one thing for me to do, and that was to make a quick couple of dollars and lead you to the altar and spend the rest of my life looking after you. Because if ever a man needed looking after, it's you. And it beats me what you're making such a fuss about. You used to be crazy about me.'

'I was young and foolish.'

'And now you're old and foolish, but all the same you're the only man I've ever wanted. It's odd, that. How does that song go? Fish gotta swim, birds gotta fly, I gotta love one man till I die. Can't help—'

'Now, Bill. Please. Listen.'

'I haven't time to listen. I'm lunching with my literary agent at the Beverly-Wilshire. He's in Hollywood for a couple of days. Who knows but what I might contrive to touch him for a hundred? In which case, I'll come back and lay it at your feet, my king.'

Smedley, a correct and fastidious dresser, who even in captivity affected Palm Beach suits of impeccable cut and crease, cast a disapproving eye at the slacks.

'You aren't going to the Beverly-Wilshire dressed like that?'

'I certainly am. And don't forget what I said about marrying you. Go off into a corner and start practising saying "I will", against the moment when the minister taps you on the chest and says: "Wilt thou, Smedley, take this Wilhelmina?" because you're for it, my lad.'

She passed through the french window on her way to the garage where her jalopy was. Her voice came booming back to him.

'Fish gotta swim, birds gotta fly, I gotta love one man till I die. Can't help lovin' that man of mine.'

Smedley Cork leaned limply against the back of the sofa, grateful for its firm support. Warm though the morning was, he shivered, as only a confirmed bachelor gazing into the naked face of matrimony can shiver.

CHAPTER 2

Joe Davenport was giving Kay Shannon lunch at the Purple Chicken down Greenwich Village way. He would much have preferred to take her to the Colony or the Pavillon, but Kay held austere views on the subject of young men wasting their substance in riotous living, even if they had recently won radio jackpots. Like her Uncle Smedley, she felt that there was no percentage in it. What Joe's stomach, which had high standards, considered a pretty revolting meal had drawn to its close, and only the last hurdle, the coffee, remained to be surmounted.

The waiter brought the coffee, breathed down the back of Joe's neck and withdrew, and Joe, who had been speaking of the lethal qualities of the management's spaghetti, abandoned the topic and turned to the one always uppermost in his mind on the occasions when he lunched with Kay.

'So much for the spaghetti theme,' he said. 'I will return to it later, if you wish. For the moment, there are weightier matters on the agenda paper. Don't look now,' said Joe, 'but will you marry me?'

Kay was leaning forward, her chin cupped in her hands and her eyes fixed on him with that grave, intent glance which always made him feel as if some hidden hand had introduced an egg whisk into his soul and started rotating it. It was this gravity of hers that had attracted him so strongly from the first. There was, he had begun to feel just before he met her, too much female smiling in this world, particularly in the cheesecake zone of Hollywood, in which until a short while before, he had had his being. It had sometimes seemed to him that his life, till Kay came into it, had become an inferno of flashing teeth and merry squeals.

'Marry you?'

'That's right.'

'You do get the oddest ideas,' said Kay.

She glanced over her shoulder. The Purple Chicken is one of those uninhibited Greenwich Village restaurants where the social amenities are not rigorously observed, and in the far corner a man who might have been a neo-Vorticist sculptor and a girl who looked as if she did bead work had begun to quarrel as loudly and cosily as if they had been at home. Turning back, she caught Joe's eye, and he frowned rebukingly.

'Don't pay any attention to those two,' he urged. 'Our marriage wouldn't be like that. They probably aren't married, anyway.'

'He seems to be talking to her like a husband.'

'Ours would be an unbroken round of bliss. Do you read Blondie? Then you will admit that the best husband in America is Dagwood Bumstead. Well, I have much in common with him – a loving heart, a gentle nature, a fondness for dogs and a taste for exotic sandwiches. Marry me, and you will be getting a super-Dagwood. Never a harsh word. Never a cross-eyed look. Your lightest wish would be law. I would bring you breakfast in bed every morning on a tray and sit and smoke to you when you had a headache.'

'It sounds wonderful. Tell me something,' said Kay. 'I notice that, when you give me lunch, you always wait till the coffee comes before proposing to me. Why is that? Just a habit?'

'On the contrary, it is very subtle stuff. Psychology. I reason that a girl full to the brim is more likely to be in softened mood than one in the process of staying the pangs of hunger. And I hate proposing with the waiters listening in and making bets in the background. Well, will you?'

'No.'

'You said that last time.'

'And I say it this time.'

'You're really turning me down again?'

'I am.'

'In spite of the fact that you are bursting with my meat?'

'I had spaghetti.'

'It makes no difference. The moral obligation of a lady bursting with a gentleman's spaghetti to do the square thing by the gentleman is equally strong.'

The sculptor and the bead worker had paid their bill and left. Freed of their distracting influence, Joe felt better able to concentrate on the matter in hand.

'It really is extraordinary,' he said, 'this way you've got of saying no every time I offer you a good man's love. No ... No ... No ... You might be Molotov. Not that it matters, of course.'

'No?'

'There you go again. I believe you say it in your sleep.'

'Why doesn't it matter, Mr Bones?'

'Because you're bound to marry me eventually, if only for my money.'

'How much have you got?'

'A thousand dollars.'

'Is that all?'

'What do you mean, is that all? I know of many a poor man who would be glad of a thousand dollars. Many a poor woman, too. Your Aunt Bill, for one.'

'I was going to say, Is that all you have left out of that jackpot?'

'Oh, well, money slips away. That has been my constant trouble as a bachelor, just as it has been Bill's constant trouble as a spinster. Have you heard from Bill lately?'

'No.'

'I had a telegram from her this morning.'

'What on earth was she telegraphing about?'

'She has some big scheme on.'

'What scheme?'

'She didn't say. The communication was rather mystic. She just spoke of her big scheme.'

'I'll bet it's crazy.'

'I'll bet it isn't. Bill crazy? The Old Reliable? As shrewd a woman as ever ate Corned Beef Hash Betty Grable at a studio commissary. Bill's a woman with ideas. When we were co-workers on the Superba-Llewellyn lot, there was a traffic cop out on Cahuenga Boulevard who lurked beside his motor cycle in a dark corner and sprang on it and dashed out to pursue motorists and give them tickets. We used to watch him from our windows, and we all burned to do something to the man, but only Bill had the vision and intelligence to go out and tie a chain to his back wheel while he was in the drug store and fasten the other end to a hydrant, so that the next time he sprang on his machine and started off, he was brought up short and shot over the handlebars and looked about as silly as I ever saw a traffic cop look. There you have Wilhelmina Shannon in a nutshell. A woman who gets things done. But to return to what I was saying, as a bachelor I have found it difficult to keep the cash from melting away. It will be different when I am married and settled down.'

'I'm not going to marry you, Joe.'

'Why not? Don't you like me?'

'You're nice to lunch with.'

'Nice is surely a weak adjective.'

The waiter was hovering in a meaning manner, and Joe, reading his thoughts, asked him for the bill. He looked across the table at Kay and felt, not for the first time, that life was very strange. You never knew what it was cooking up for you. When, as he was leaving Hollywood, Bill Shannon had told him to get in touch with her niece Kay in New York, where she was working in a magazine office, he had done so, he remembered, purely to oblige good old Bill. A young man who never lacked for feminine society, he had anticipated small pleasure or profit from adding one more to the list of telephone numbers in his little red book. But Bill had told him to get in touch, so he had got in touch. And from that simple, kindly act, had resulted all these emotional earthquakes which were upsetting him so deplorably.

'Bill ought to have warned me what I was coming up against,' said Joe, pursuing this train of thought. ' "When you hit New York," she said, "go and say Hello to my niece Kay." Like that. Casual. Off-hand. Not a suggestion that she was introducing into my life a girl with a heart of stone who would disorganize my whole existence and turn me into a nervous wreck. Talk about La Belle Dame Sans Merci.'

'Keats!' said Kay, surprised. 'A well-read young man, this. I must try to get his autograph. I didn't know you went in for poetry.'

'All the time. Whenever I have a spare half-hour, you will generally find me curled up with Keats's *latest*. "Ah, what can ail thee, wretched wight, alone and palely loitering?" I tell you,' said Joe, 'if that wretched wight were to walk into this restaurant at this moment, beefing about La Belle Dame Sans Merci having him in thrall, I would slap him on the back and tell him I knew just how he felt.'

'Though, of course, he was a lot worse off than you are.'

'How do you make that out?'

'He didn't have a little red book of telephone numbers.'

Joe started and, though most of his friends would have said that such a thing was impossible, blushed.

'What do you know about my little red book?'

'You left it on the table once when you went to speak to someone. I glanced idly through it. Who are they all?'

'Chunks of my dead past.'

'M'm.'

'Don't say M'm. Those girls mean nothing to me. Ghosts, that's what they are. Just so much flotsam and jetsam left stranded by the tide on the beach of memory. Bring any one of them to me on a plate with watercress around her, and I wouldn't so much as touch her hand. Nobody but you exists for me now. Don't you believe me?'

'No.'

'That word again. By the beard of Sam Goldwyn, there are moments when I feel an almost overpowering urge to bean you with a bottle.'

Kay raised her coffee spoon.

'Stand back. I am armed.'

'Oh, it's all right. I'm not going to. I would only get hell from Emily Post.'

The waiter brought the bill, and Joe paid it absently. Kay was looking at him again in that odd, speculative way of hers.

'It isn't the little red book that worries me,' she said. 'If you're a reformed Casanova, that's fine. Shall I tell you the reason why I won't marry you, Joe?'

'I wish you would. Clear up this historic mystery.'

'I'll only be saying what you know already.'

'That's all right. Just so long as you talk about me.'

Kay took a sip of coffee, found that it had become cold and put the cup down. The restaurant had emptied, the waiters retired to some secret lair of their own. She could speak without being overheard.

'Well, then, it's because you're not what the French call an *homme sérieux*. If you know what that means.'

'I don't.'

'I'll try to explain. Let's just run through your case history. I had it from Bill. She said that when you and she were in New York, before you both went to Hollywood, you were doing quite well as a writer.'

'For the pulps. '

'Well, what's wrong with that? Half the best known writers today started on the pulps. But they stuck to it and worked.'

'I don't like the way you said that.'

'Then you got a job with Superba-Llewellyn and went to Hollywood. Then you got fired.'

'It happens to everybody.'

'Yes, but most people when they get fired don't ask for a personal interview with the boss of the studio and in the course of conversation throw a richly bound copy of the *Saturday Evening Post* at his head. What made you do that?'

'It seemed a good idea at the time. He had incurred my displeasure. Did Bill tell you about it?'

'Yes.'

'Bill talks too much.'

'So you got yourself blacklisted. Not very balanced behaviour, do you think?'

Joe patted her hand indulgently.

'Women don't understand these things,' he said. 'There comes a time in the life of every man placed in juxtaposition with Ivor Llewellyn when he is compelled to throw copies of the *Saturday Evening Post* at his head. It's why they publish the *Saturday Evening Post*.'

'Well, all right. I still think it was unbalanced, but if you say so, all right. We now come to the matter of that radio jackpot. When you get a lot of money by a miracle, winning a radio jackpot—'

Joe, though saddened by the turn the conversation had taken, was obliged to chuckle.

'I always get a hearty laugh out of that,' he said. 'I'm sitting in my squalid flat one rainy evening, feeling extremely dubious as to the whereabouts of my next meal, when the telephone tinkles and a hearty character at Station W.J.Z. asks me to listen to a Mysterious Voice on a record and see if I can identify it. And whose mysterious voice is it? None other than that of Mr Ivor Llewellyn, which had been ringing in my ears ever since that episode to which you have alluded. Having identified it, I am informed by the hearty character that I have won the big jackpot and scooped in wealth beyond the dreams of avarice. It just shows that nothing is put into this world without a purpose, not even Ivor Llewellyn. But I interrupt you.'

'You do.'

'I'm sorry. Carry on. You were saying—?'

'I was saying that the first thing you do when by a miracle you get a lot of money is to stop writing and just loaf.'

'You wrong me.'

'Have you written a single story since you won that money?'

'No. But I've not been loafing. I've been looking about me, crouching for the spring. The view I take is that there must be something better for me to do than hammer out cowboy stories for the pulp magazines. Now that I have a bit of capital, I can afford to wait and study the market. That's what I'm doing, studying the market.'

'I see. Well,' said Kay, getting up, 'I must be going. And I still stick to it that you're not an *homme sérieux.*'

A feeling of desolation swept over Joe. It had been there in a modified form all the time, but it was only now that he actually seemed to realize that in a few days he would be separated from this girl by three thousand miles of mountain and desert and prairie. And if ever there was a job that called for uninterrupted personal supervision, it was this job of breaking down Kay Shannon's customer's sales resistance.

'Oh, don't go yet,' he said.

'I must. I've a hundred things to do.'

'Heavy day at the office?'

'I'm packing. My vacation starts tomorrow.'

'You never told me that.'

'I suppose it slipped my mind.'

'Where are you going?'

'Hollywood. What's the matter?'

'Nothing's the matter.'

'You barked like a seal.'

'I always bark like a seal at about this hour. So you're going to Hollywood?'

'Well, Beverly Hills. I'm going to stay with my aunt.'

'Bill?'

'No, this is another one. Bill's sister. Much higher in the social scale than Bill. She's one of the old aristocracy of Hollywood. Adela Shannon.'

'What, *the* Adela Shannon? The silent film star?'

'That's the one.'

'I've heard Bill speak of her. Bill didn't seem to like her much.'

'I don't like her much myself.'

'Then why are you going to stay with her?'

'Oh, I don't know. One must go somewhere. She invited me.'

'Where does she live?'

'Up in the mountains at the top of Alamo Drive. What used to be the Carmen Flores place. You probably know it.'

'She owns that palace, does she? She must have plenty of money.'

'She has. She married a millionaire.'

'You'll be doing the same thing yourself, if I find my niche and really get going. Well, expect an early phone call from me.'

'Expect a what?'

Joe laughed. His depression had vanished. The sun had broken through the clouds and all was for the best in this best of all possible worlds.

'Did you think to escape me by running off to Hollywood? Girl, you have been living in a fool's paradise. I'm going there myself in a couple of days.'

'What! But you're blacklisted in Hollywood.'

'Oh, I'm not going to work there. No doubt they will come begging me to, but I shall draw myself up and say: "Not after what has occurred." And I shall say it stiffly. No, I'm going to confer with Bill about this scheme of hers. Rightly or wrongly, she seems to think that my co-operation is needed to make it a success. She was very emphatic that I must drop everything and come running. It's a pity we won't be able to travel together, but there are one or two things I have to do before I can leave the metropolis. However, you will be hearing from me in due season. In fact, you'll be seeing me.'

'You aren't thinking of strolling in on Aunt Adela?'

'I might.'

'I wouldn't.'

'She can't eat me.'

'I don't know so much. She's not a vegetarian.'

'Well, we will see, we will see. And as regards the matter which we have been discussing, we will leave things as they are for the time being. I shall continue to love you, of course.'

'Thanks.'

'Not at all,' said Joe. 'A pleasure. It'll be something to do.'

'Hollywood,' said Bill Shannon, 'is not the place it used to be. Hollywood,' said Bill, 'once a combination of Santa Claus and Good King Wenceslas, has turned into a Scrooge. The dear old days are dead and the spirit of cheerful giving a thing of the past.'

She was sharing a pot of coffee with Joe Davenport in the main dining-room of the Beverly Hills hotel, and her resonant voice rang through it like rolling thunder. Listening to her, Joe felt as if he were a section of the voting public being harangued by a Senator of more than ordinary lung power.

'Why, look,' said Bill. 'There was a time when only a person of exceptional ability and determination could keep from getting signed by a studio. Top level executives used to chase you along Sunset Boulevard, pleading pitifully with you to accept a contract. "Come and write for us," they begged, and when you told them you weren't a writer, they said: "Well, come and be a technical adviser." And when you said you didn't want to be a technical adviser, they said: "Then come and be a vocal instructor." So you said: "Oh, all right, I'll be a writer. I shall want fifteen hundred a week." "Or two thousand?" they said. "It's a rounder figure. Simplifies book-keeping." And you said: "Oh, very well, two thousand. But don't expect me to do any work!" And they said: "Of course not, of course not. What an idea! We just want to have you around the place." But all that is over. Now? Ha! Nowadays, if they sign you up at all, it's just to have the fun of firing you.'

All this was in response to Joe's casual question 'Well, how's dear old Hollywood?' and he felt like someone who has thoughtlessly punched a hole in a dam. Overcoming the dazed sensation of being a twig tossed along on foaming waters, he found himself able to guess at the cause of his companion's emotion.

'Don't tell me they've handed you the black spot, Bill.'

'That's what they've done. Driven me out into the snow. And I always thought they looked on me as the Little Mother around the place. A sort of studio mascot.'

'When did this happen?'

'Last week. I dance into my office with my hat on the side of my head, singing "I'm to be Queen of the May, mother, I'm to be Queen of the May", and there on the desk the brusheroo in its little blue envelope. A most unpleasant shock, you can take it from me. I had to go off to the commissary and restore myself with a Malted Milk Bette Davis.'

Joe nodded understandingly.

'It's this economy wave.'

'False economy.'

'I suppose Hollywood's in a pretty bad way these days?'

'Down to its last billion.'

'One might have expected that something like that would happen when they let me go. A suicidal policy. What are you going to do?'

'For the moment, I'm staying with my sister Adela. I'm ghostwriting the story of her life. By the way, Kay clocked in a day or two ago. Did you see anything of her in New York?'

Joe laughed one of those hollow, mirthless laughs.

'Did I see anything of her in New York! The answer to your question, Wilhelmina, is in the affirmative. My misguided old friend, you little knew what you were letting me in for when you told me to go and say Hello to that girl. Lowered morale. Depression and debility. Night sweats and loss of appetite. I love her, Bill.'

'You do?'

'I do.'

'Well, I don't know that I blame you. She's an attractive young squirt.'

'I would prefer that you did not allude to her as a squirt. An angel, if you like. A seraph, if you wish. But not a squirt.'

'Just as you say. And how's it all coming along? Does she respond? Are you her dream man?'

'To use a favourite word of her own, no.'

'She won't marry you?'

'That's her story.'

'Ask her again.'

'I have asked her again. How do you think I fill in the time? I've asked her twelve times. No, sorry, fourteen. I overlooked a couple of small ones. The score would be fifteen if I had been able to get her on the phone just now, but she was out. Bill, who would a Mrs Cork be?'

'My sister Adela. She married a well-to-do millionaire of that name. Why?'

'I was just wondering. We exchanged a word or two over the wire. Well, that's how matters stand. I keep proposing to her, and she steadfastly continues to be a black frost in my garden of dreams. So now you know why I look pale and wan.'

'You look like a particularly healthy tomato. And you're crazy if you pay any attention to a girl when she says no. I'm in love with a man who's been saying no for the last twenty years. But do I despair? Not by a jugful. I keep after him, and I think I'm softening him up. What are you goggling like that for?'

Joe hesitated.

'Well, I'm sort of surprised.'

'Why?'

'I somehow didn't associate you with the tender passion.'

'Why not?'

'Or, rather,' said Joe, catching his companion's eye, which had begun to look menacing, 'it astonished me that anyone could resist you for twenty years.'

'That's better.'

'I think you'll get him. Persevere, Bill.'

'I will. And you persevere, too.'

'Right. Let's all persevere.'

'We'll make it a double wedding.'

'That's the spirit.'

'And now, for heaven's sake, let's change the subject and get down to business. We can't waste the whole day talking about love. You got my telegram?'

'That's why I'm here.'

'And my letter, giving you full details of this scheme of mine?'

'I never got any letter.'

'And I'll tell you why. I've just remembered I forgot to mail it. But I can supply you with all the facts now. My boy, we're on the eve of making a stupendous fortune. We've got a gold mine.'

'Proceed, Bill. You interest me strangely.'

Bill tapped his chest with an impressive finger.

'Has it ever occurred to you, Joe, that all these years you and I have been in this writing game on the wrong end?'

'How do you mean, the wrong end?'

'The loser's end. The sap's end. We've been perfect suckers. Where is it getting us, toiling for the pulps and being wage slaves in Hollywood? Nowhere.'

'So—?'

'So we're going to be literary agents.'

'Eh?'

'I should say authors' representatives. It sounds better. We're going to loll back and let the other fellows do the work and take our ten per cent like officers and gentlemen.'

'What has given you that idea?'

'It came to me like a flash the other afternoon when I was lunching with my personal bloodsucker, who has been putting in a few days in Screwball Centre. I had noticed from the first that the man seemed nervous and depressed, and just after I had touched him for a couple of hundred dollars during the smoked salmon course he suddenly buried his face in his hands with a low groan and said that this was the finish. It couldn't go on, he said. He had got to retire, he said. He said he had reached a point where he never wanted to see an author again. He said authors did something to him. He said he supposed Providence had had some sort of idea at the back of its mind when it put authors into the world, but he had never been able to figure out what it was, and he pined for a quiet evening of his life in some remote spot like the Virgin Islands, where he could reasonably hope to be free from them. So, to condense a novelette into a short-short, I arranged with him to give me first refusal of the goodwill and effects, or whatever they're called. But we've got to act like lightning, because a week from now, if we haven't clinched the deal, he will go elsewhere. So now is the time for all good men to come to the aid of the party.'

Joe found himself a good deal infected by her enthusiasm. The thought of becoming an authors' representative had not presented itself to him before, but he could see now that it was just the sort of thing he had been subconsciously looking for when studying the market. Like all writers, he had long held the view that of all the soft snaps in this modern civilization of ours that of the authors' representative was the softest. Given the modest intelligence necessary for putting a typescript in an envelope and licking the gum, a man could scarcely fail in that branch of industry. Whoever went around in patched clothes with holes in his shoes and had to skip a meal from time to time, it was not the authors' representative.

He had begun to weave an opalescent daydream in which Kay, learning that he had become one of that opulent little band who represent authors, flung herself weeping on his chest, remorseful that she had ever wronged him by failing to classify him as what the French call an *homme sérieux*, when Bill continued her remarks.

'He's asking twenty thousand.'

Joe's daydream broke into fragments like a soup-plate coming apart in the hands of a careless scullery maid. He gave a soft gurgle, and when he spoke, spoke in a low, grating voice.

'Twenty thousand?'

'That's all. He started by talking some wild, visionary stuff about thirty, but I soon put a stop to that.'

'You expect to get twenty thousand dollars?'

'Why not?'

'Which bank are you going to burgle?'

Joe shrank back in his chair. Wilhelmina Shannon was raising her voice again.

'What do you mean, which bank am I going to burgle? I'm

looking to you to put up the capital. Aren't you putrescent with money?'

'I've a thousand dollars, if you call that putrescent.'

'A thousand? What's become of that radio jackpot?'

'Gone with the wind.'

'You dissolute young rat.'

'High cost of living, taxes and so on. And a thing you're over-looking, Bill, is that these radio jackpots aren't solid cash. Don't be misled by what you read in the papers. Most of mine was tinned soup. Would this man of yours settle for eight thousand tins of mixed soups? Maybe he's fond of soup. I could do him tomato, asparagus, green pea, chicken gumbo . . .'

An old gentleman who was drinking something through a straw at a table at the other end of the room leaped convulsively and nearly swallowed the straw. This was because Bill was raising her voice still higher.

'So one more dream turns blue,' said Bill. 'Can you direct me to a good Old Women's Home?'

Her anguish touched Joe. His was a resilient nature, and already he had begun to recover from the gloom into which he had been plunged.

'Don't be a defeatist, Bill. Why shouldn't we raise the money somewhere?'

'Where?'

'There used to be a place called Perelli's down at Santa Monica where one could engage in games of chance. I presume it still exists. I might take my thousand and look in there tonight.'

'Don't be a fool.'

'Perhaps you're right. Well, why shouldn't we float a loan in some quarter? Hollywood must be full of rich sportsmen who would like a flutter.'

'I've never met them.'

'What about Mrs Cork?'

'Adela? The slowest woman with a dollar west of Dodge City. No, this is the end. Doom, desolation and despair. Well, see you in the breadline,' said Bill, and moved ponderously to the door, a female Napoleon retreating from Moscow.

For some minutes after she had left him, Joe sat musing on the capriciousness of fate, which lures you on with golden promises and then turns round and lets you have it on the base of the skull with the stuffed eelskin. But his, as has been said, was a resilient nature, and it was not long before there began to glimmer through the cloud wrack a small but distinct silver lining. It might be that he would have to postpone becoming a millionaire for a while, but money is not everything and the world, he reminded himself, though admittedly grey in spots, still contained the girl he loved. And by chartering a yellow taxi from the stand outside the Marion Hunter bookshop and going to the top of Alamo Drive, he could feast his eyes on the house where she was in residence. With a little luck, he might even catch a glimpse of her.

Twenty minutes later, seated in a yellow taxi, he was gazing out of the window at a broad gateway and a tree-lined strip of concrete drive which led to a house unfortunately invisible from where he sat. He felt like some pilgrim visiting a shrine, and mingled with his reverence was the earthier feeling that when Mrs Adela Cork had taken a millionaire for a husband, she had picked a good one. The grounds, he could see, were spacious and expensive, and when there suddenly appeared, crossing the drive with a tray of cocktails, what was plainly an imported English butler, any doubt that he might have had as to this being one of the Stately Homes of Hollywood was dispelled.

It was probably the sight of those cocktails that suggested to him that it was about time to be getting back and making arrangements for dinner. The California evening had mellowed to twilight, and his stomach, always inclined to the policy of Do It Now, was sending up peremptory messages to the front office. Reluctantly, for he regretted the necessity of yielding to his lower nature, he was about to notify the charioteer that the homeward journey might commence, when along the drive and out of the gate came toddling a large, stout, elderly gentleman who looked like a Roman Emperor who has been doing himself too well on the starchy foods, and so impressive was his exterior that it immediately occurred to Joe that here, first crack out of the box, he had found the very man of whom he was in search, one of those big shots who feed sums like twenty thousand dollars to the birds.

For to Joe, meeting him here, it was obvious who this was. It could be none other than the plutocrat Cork, the super-tax-paying mate of Kay's Aunt Adela. You had only to cast an eye on the man to see that he had the stuff in sackfuls. It is difficult to explain exactly, but there is something about these very rich men which marks them off from the common herd. They look different. The way they walk is different. They say: 'Hey, taxi!' differently.

This was what the other was now saying and for a moment Joe was puzzled that such an Crœsus should be hailing taxis. Then he saw that the explanation was quite simple. Something – trivial, one hoped – must have gone temporarily wrong with the Lincoln, the Cadillac and the two Rolls-Royces in his garage.

His lightning mind perceived that here was a heaven-sent opportunity of fraternizing with this gilt-edged security and starting a beautiful friendship.

'I am going to Beverly Hills, sir,' he said, poking his head out of the window, full of charm. 'Could I give you a lift, sir?'

'Very kind of you, sir.'

'Not at all, sir.'

'Thank you, sir.'

'Don't give it a thought, sir. Hop in, sir, hop in.'

The taxi rolled off down the mountain-side, and Joe braced himself to be fascinating.

CHAPTER 4

The midday sun, pouring into the Garden Room on the follow-ing morning, found Bill Shannon seated at the desk, the dicta-phone tube in her hand, a peevish frown on her face. One would have said that she was not enjoying working on the *Memoirs* of her sister Adela, and one would have been right. Bill in her time had been many things, crime reporter, sob sister, writer of stories for the pulp magazines, Press agent, minor actress and baby sitter, but this was the most uncongenial task which she had ever undertaken.

As far as she could ascertain from the voluminous notes which the heroine of the *Memoirs* had placed at her disposal, nothing had ever happened to Adela that was of the remotest interest to anyone except herself. She had apparently never done anything in all her years of silent stardom but eat, sleep, get married, and have her photograph taken. It was not easy to see how the Adela Shannon Story could be stretched to cover three hundred pages of entertaining reading for the American public.

But Bill was conscientious and resolved to give of her best, and it was with splendid determination that she ignored the sunshine that was trying to lure her out into the open spaces.

'It was all so new and strange,' she boomed into the mouth-piece, 'and I was just a timid little tot ... Oh, dammit, I've used timid little tot before … and I was so young, so unsophisticated, so dazzled and bewildered by the glitter and glamour of this world … No, we want some adjectives there … of this strange, new, magic world into which I had been plunged … Oh, blast it, I said new and strange a moment ago … of this marvellous, magical, fairyland world into which I had plunged like a diver diving into some rushing, sparkling stream. Who could have dreamed—'

Phipps came shimmering through the door, in his capable hands a whisky and soda on a tray. She welcomed him with a glad cry like that of a diver diving into some rushing, sparkling stream who finds the water warmer than she had expected. No Israelite in the desert, watching manna descending from the skies just when he had been saying to himself how well a spot of manna would go down right now, if only he had it, could have shown a more instantaneous approval and enthusiasm.

'Phipps, you're a mind reader.'

'I thought you might be in need of refreshment, madam. You have been working all the morning.'

'And no interruptions, thank heaven. Where is everybody?'

'Mrs Cork went to Pasadena, madam, to address a ladies club on "Some Recollections of the Silent Screen". Miss Kay and his lordship are playing golf.'

'And Mr Smedley?'

'I have not seen Mr Smedley, madam.'

'Probably around somewhere.'

'No doubt, madam.'

Bill took a sip and a swallow and composed herself for conversation. She had reached a point in her labours when she was glad of the interruption which would have irked her earlier, and she was particularly glad to be interrupted by Phipps. This butler intrigued her. Since their get-together of the previous day, she had been thinking not a little about his curious case.

'I wish you would explain something that's been puzzling me, Phipps.'

'Certainly, madam, if it is within my power.'

Bill addressed herself to the glass again. Its amber contents were cool and refreshing. She lit a cigarette and blew a puff of smoke at a fly which had wandered in and was circling about her head.

'It's this,' she said, putting the question which she hoped would lead to a solution of the mystery which had been vexing her. 'You remember – how shall I put it, always bearing in mind that walls have ears – you remember that lawsuit of yours?'

'Yes, madam.'

'The one where I was a member of the jury.'

'Yes, madam.'

Bill discouraged the fly with another broadside.

'Well, here's where I can't get the thing straight. It seemed to me that on that occasion, and the rest of the boys and girls felt the same, that the gentleman who was digging up the details of your past and dishing them out to the intelligent twelve, of whom I was one, established rather clearly that you were an expert safeblower.'

'Yes, madam.'

'And it didn't take me long after I'd got here to see that you were certainly an expert butler.'

'Thank you, madam.'

'Well, which came first, the chicken or the egg?'

'Madam?'

Bill saw that she had not made herself clear.

'I mean, are you a safeblower—'

'An ex-safeblower, madam.'

'You're sure you spell it with an ex?'

'Oh, yes, madam.'

'Well, be that as it may, are you a safeblower magically gifted with the art of buttling, or a butler who has somehow picked up the knack of blowing safes?'

'The latter, madam.'

'You aren't really Mike the Mugg or something like that, just posing as a butler for your own subtle ends?'

'Oh, no, madam. I have been in service from a very early age. Domestic service is a tradition in my family. I started my career as what is known as a hall boy in a large establishment in Worcestershire.'

'Where the sauce comes from?'

'I believe the condiment to which you allude is manufactured in that locality, madam.'

Phipps stood silent for a moment, his thoughts apparently back in those happy days when life had been simple and free from problems and complexities. Apart from having to carry logs of wood up stairs and deposit them in bedrooms, hall boys in English houses have it pretty soft.

'In due course,' he proceeded, coming out of his reverie, 'I rose to be an under footman, then a footman and finally a butler. And it was after I had achieved that position that I entered the employment of an American gentleman and came to this country. I had always had a desire to visit the United States of Northern America. That was some ten years ago.'

'And when did you learn to bust safes?'

'About five years after that, madam.'

'What gave you the idea?'

Phipps looked cautiously over his shoulder. Having done this, he directed a searching glance at Bill, as if he were weighing her in the balance. He seemed to be asking himself whether it would be wise and judicious to confide in a woman who, though of course they knew each other quite well by sight, was after all a stranger. Then the benevolence of his companion's rugged face overcame his doubts. There was that about Bill Shannon which always encouraged people to confide in her.

'It came to me quite unexpectedly one evening when I was reading a volume entitled *Three Dead At Midways Court*, madam. I have always been fond of that type of literature, and in the course of my perusal of these fictional works – known, I believe, as whodunits – I was struck by the frequency with which the butler proved to be the criminal.'

'I know what you mean. It's always the butler. It's an occupational disease.'

'What is termed the Heavy in *Three Dead At Midways Court* turned out to be the butler, and until the final chapter nobody had suspected him for a moment. It started a train of thought. I mused, madam. Butlers, I told myself, never are suspected for a moment, and it occurred to me that a butler in a wealthy household who had acquired the technique of opening safes would be very advantageously placed. There he would be, if you follow me, madam, with the valuables at his elbow, if I may use the expression, and it would be extremely simple for him, by leaving a window open, to invest his operations with the appearance of what is known as an outside job. So to cut a long story short, madam, I made cautious inquiries and eventually found a practitioner in Brooklyn who in return for a fee was willing to impart his skill to me.'

'In twelve easy lessons?'

'Twenty, madam. At first I was not a very apt pupil.'

'But you picked it up all right as you went along?'

'Yes, madam.'

Bill drew a deep breath. She was no rigid moralist, her temperament being one that always inclined her to take a tolerant view of the straying from the straight and narrow path of those with whom she associated, but she had a rudimentary conscience. And though she had never been fond of her sister Adela, she could not but feel that a word of warning should be given that exasperating woman. The generosity of the late Albert Cork, combined with her personal and private fortune, the outcome of years of pulling down a huge salary in the days before there was any income tax to speak of, had left Adela with enough jewellery to equip half the blondes in Hollywood, and it seemed unfair to allow her to go on giving board and lodging to a butler who, as had been established in court, could open safes with a twiddle of his finger tips.

'I ought to tell Mrs Cork,' she said.

'There is no necessity, madam. I have put all that sort of thing behind me.'

'Says you, if I may use a homely phrase indicating doubt and uncertainty.'

'No, madam, I assure you. Apart from the moral aspect of the matter, I would not dream of taking upon myself the risks inseparable from my former activities. My experience of American prison life has left me with no desire to repeat it.'

Bill's face cleared. This was sense.

'I see what you mean. I remember reading an article in the *Yale Review* about the Reformed Criminal. The writer pointed out that there is nobody with such a strong bias toward honesty as the man who has just come out of prison. He said that if someone had been laid up for a year in hospital as the result of going over Niagara Falls in a barrel, the one outdoor sport in which he would be reluctant to indulge on emerging would be going over Niagara Falls in a barrel. Or, putting it another way, the burned child fears the fire.'

'Precisely, madam, though the actual quotation is "A burned child dreadeth the fire." It occurs in Lyly's *Euphues*.'

'Is that a favourite bedside book of yours?'

'I glanced through it, madam, when I was in the service of the Earl of Powick, in Worcestershire. There was very little else to read in his lordship's library, and it rained a good deal.'

'I've come up against that sort of thing myself. I once went to Valparaiso as a stewardess on a fruit boat, and the only book on board was *The Plays of William Shakespeare*, belonging to the chief engineer. By the time the voyage was over, I knew them by heart. I suppose that's why I quote him a good deal.'

'No doubt, madam. A very admirable writer.'

'Yes, he wrote some good stuff. But tell me all about your college days, Phipps. What's it like in Sing...?'

'Hist, madam.'

'How do you mean, hist? Oh, I get you.'

Outside the french window a voice had suddenly made itself heard, singing a gay melody. A moment later, a long, lean young man, who appeared to have giraffe blood in him, came in, carrying a bag of golf clubs. Phipps greeted him with respectful devotion.

'Good morning, m'lord.'

'Good morning, Lord Topham,' said Bill.

'Oh, good morning,' said the young man. Then, as if to clarify his meaning, he added the words 'Good morning, good morning, good morning!' He beamed at Bill and the butler. 'Well, Miss W. Shannon,' he proceeded, 'and you, Phipps, this is the maddest, merriest day of all the glad new year. I say this to you without reserve, Phipps, and you, Miss W. Shannon. Not only the maddest, but also the merriest day of the glad new year. I broke a hundred this morning, a feat which has eluded my every effort since I first took driver in hand at the age of twenty. A whisky and soda would not come amiss, Phippsy. You might take it to my room.'

'Very good, m'lord,' said Phipps. 'I will attend to the matter immediately.'

Lord Topham gazed after him admiringly as he disappeared in the stately manner habitual with him.

'You know, that chap makes me feel homesick. Absolutely. I never expected to find an English butler in Hollywood.'

'All sorts of English oddities turn up in Hollywood,' said Bill. 'Excuse me.' She picked up the mouthpiece of the dictaphone and began speaking into it. 'Who could have dreamed that in a few short years the name of Adela Shannon would have been known to the whole wide world from China to Peru? Who would have supposed that before I made my third picture, I would have become loved, worshipped, idolized by the prince in his palace, the peasant in his cot, the explorer in the jungle and the Eskimo in his frozen igloo? So true it is – so true— Ha!' said Bill. 'So true it is that one touch of nature makes the whole world kin and that courage, patience and perseverance will always find a way. I will now describe my first meeting with Nick Schenk.' She lowered the instrument. 'Sorry,' she said. 'I have to jot these things down when the inspiration comes.'

Lord Topham was impressed, as the layman always is when privileged to observe genius in the throes of composition.

'Oh, absolutely,' he agreed. 'What was that about glue?'

'Igloo. It's a sort of gloo they have up in the Arctic circle.'

'I see.'

'Stickier than the usual kind.'

'Quite. What are you doing? Working on a picture?'

'Not on a picture, no. I'm ghostwriting the story of my sister Adela's life.'

'How's it coming?'

'Not too smoothly.'

'Pretty much of a somewhat ghastly sweat, I imagine. I couldn't write anything if you paid me, much less talk it into that sewing-machine thing. Mrs Cork was a big pot in the silent films, wasn't she?'

'One of the biggest. They called her the Empress of Stormy Emotion.'

'Must have made a lot of money.'

'Quite a good deal.'

'I mean, you don't get a house like this for nothing.'

'No. But here she is, to give you all the figures, if you want them.'

The door which led to the main portion of the house had opened, and a strikingly handsome woman of about Bill's age was sailing in with that air of confidence and authority which is so noticeable in Empresses of Stormy Emotion, even when the passage of time has made them ex-Empresses. Adela Cork was tall and stately, with large, dark, slumberous eyes which could and did, light up in a baleful blaze when things were not going exactly as she desired. She had something of the imperious look of those portraits of Louise de Querouaille which make the beholder feel what a man of steely nerve King Charles the Second must have been to associate on terms of intimacy with anything so formidable. Formidable was the word to describe Bill's sister Adela. Each of her three husbands, even the late Alfred Cork, who was as tough a citizen as ever owned an oil well, had curled up before her like carbon paper: and directors who were getting on in years sometimes woke trembling in the night, having dreamed that they were back in the pre-talkie days arguing some technical point with the former Adela Shannon.

At the moment, her mood was reasonably benevolent, though she proposed later on to have a word with Bill about those slacks. Her lecture had been well received, and she was still in the gentle glow of amiability induced by the applause of two hundred intelligent Pasadena matrons.

'Good morning,' she said. 'Good morning, Lord Topham.'

'Good morning, good morning, good morning, good morning.'

'Hello, Adela,' said Bill. 'Lord Topham was just saying how much he admired this house.'

Adela smiled rewardingly on this worthy guest. She was fond and proud of Lord Topham. She had been to great trouble to extract him from the clutches of a prehensile hostess who had seemed at one time to have acquired permanent possession, and her attitude toward him was a little like that of a collector toward a valuable piece of bric-à-brac which he has wrested from a rival connoisseur.

'It is nice, isn't it? I bought it just as it stood from the estate of Carmen Flores, the Mexican star who was killed in that plane crash last year.'

Lord Topham was interested. He was a great reader of *Screen Topics, Screen Secrets* and other organs of that nature.

'Oh, really? Carmen Flores, what? Fancy that.'

'You have heard of Carmen Flores?'

'Absolutely. Well, I mean to say, one would, wouldn't one? She, as it were, lives in legend and song. By way of being what Americans call a red-hot mother, was she not?'

'Absolutely,' said Bill. 'I have often thought that if walls had tongues as well as ears . . . Walls do have ears. Did you know that?'

'No, really?'

'Absolutely,' said Bill. 'I had it from a reliable source. Well, as I was saying, I have often thought that if walls could speak, these walls could say a mouthful. Not that what they said would ever get past the Johnston office.'

'Absolutely not,' said Lord Topham, nodding sagely. 'So this is where she lived, is it? Well, well. Who knows but that on that very sofa— I forget what I was going to say.'

'Just in time,' said Bill. 'Quickly changing the subject, tell Adela about your triumphs on the links this morning.'

Lord Topham required no coaxing.

'Oh, ah, yes. I broke a hundred, Mrs Cork. Do you play golf?' he asked, though a glance at his hostess should have told him that it was a foolish question. Women like Adela Cork do not lower themselves to these trivial pastimes. With a stretch of imagination one could picture Mrs Siddons or the mother of the Gracchi playing golf, but not Adela.

'No,' she said. 'I do not.'

'Oh! Well, the idea of the game is to bash the old ball round the course in a minimum of strokes, and anyone who can accomplish the enterprise in under a hundred bashes is entitled to credit and respect. I did it for the first time this morning, and the news will stun my circle of friends across the sea. If you'll excuse me, I'll be going and telling old Twingo about it.'

'Twingo?'

'A pal of mine in London. May I use your telephone? Thanks awfully,' said Lord Topham, and hastened out to shoot the hot news across the Atlantic.

Bill smiled sardonically.

'Pal of mine in London ... May I use your telephone ... Just like that.'

Adela bridled. She resented criticism of her favoured guest.

'Very rich men don't bother about these trifles. Lord Topham is one of the richest men in England.'

'I'm not surprised. His personal expenses must be very small.'

'And I do wish, Wilhelmina,' said Adela, changing the subject, 'that you would dress decently when you are in a civilized house. Slopping about in those slacks. You look perfectly revolting. What do you suppose Lord Topham thinks?'

'Does he think?'

'Dungarees!' said Adela, wrinkling her nose with distaste.

Bill was one of the few people whom Adela Cork could not intimidate.

'Never mind about my dungarees,' she said. 'Just tell yourself that they cover a warm heart and let it go at that. How was your lecture? Did you massacre them?'

'It was a great success. Everybody most enthusiastic.'

'You're back early. Couldn't you touch the girls for lunch?'

Adela clicked her tongue.

'My dear Wilhelmina, have you forgotten that I am giving a big luncheon party today? All sorts of important people are coming, including Jacob Glutz.'

'Of Medulla-Oblongata-Glutz? The man who looks like a lobster?'

'He does not look like a lobster.'

'Pardon me, he looks much more like a lobster than most lobsters do.'

'Well, whatever he looks like, I don't want him mistaking you for one of the gardeners. I trust you intend to change into something reasonably respectable before he arrives.'

'Of course. These are just my working clothes.'

'Have you been working on the *Memoirs*?'

'All the morning.'

'Where have you got to?'

'Your first meeting with Nick Schenk.'

'No further than that?'

Bill felt that this sort of thing must be checked at the outset. It was bad enough being compelled by poverty to write those *Memoirs* at all, without having Adela biting at her heels and baying after her like a bloodhound. A pang shot through her as she thought of that literary agency, now gone beyond recall.

'My good woman,' she said, 'be reasonable. The story of your great career will be a very important contribution to American literature. It is not a task that can be hurried. One proceeds slowly. One chisels and polishes. You don't suppose Lytton Strachey raced through his *Life of Queen Victoria* like a Bowery bum charging into a saloon for a quick beer?'

'I see. Yes, I suppose you're right.'

'You bet I'm right. I was saying to Kay yesterday— What's the matter?'

Adela had uttered an exclamation. She was looking cautiously over her shoulder. It seemed to Bill that her life these last days had been passed exclusively in the society of people who looked cautiously over their shoulders. She watched her sister, mystified, as she went to the door, opened it quickly and peered out.

'I thought Phipps might be listening,' said Adela, closing the door and coming back into the room. 'Wilhelmina, there is something I want to ask you. About Kay.'

'What about her?'

Adela sank her voice to a stage whisper.

'Has she ever spoken to you of anyone called *Joe*?'

'Joe?'

'I'll tell you why I ask. Yesterday afternoon the telephone rang as I was coming through the hall. I answered it, and a man's voice said "Kay? This is Joe. Stop me if you've heard this before, but will you marry me?"'

Bill clicked her tongue.

'The boy's crazy. That's no way to—'

'I said: "You are speaking to Mrs Cork," and he said "Oops! Sorry!" and rang off. Have you any idea who it could have been?'

Bill was able to supply the information.

'I can tell you who it must certainly have been. A young writer of my acquaintance named Joe Davenport. We were at Superba-Llewellyn together till he got fired. Shipped out to Hollywood at the same time in a crate of twelve. There is nothing surprising in the fact that he should have been asking Kay to marry him. I believe he does it every hour on the hour. He loves her with a fervour you don't often see off the Superba-Llewellyn lot.'

'Great heavens!'

'Why? Don't you approve of young love in springtime?'

'Not between my niece and a Hollywood writer who hasn't even got a job.'

'Joe may be out of a job, but he has a glittering future, if he can find some sporting soul to lend him twenty thousand dollars. If he had the capital, he could buy a lucrative Authors' Representativery. Would you care to lend him twenty thousand dollars?'

'I would not. Is Kay in love with this man?'

'Well, she gives a sort of rippling laugh, a kind of amused tee-hee, whenever I mention his name. Maybe that's a good sign. I must consult Dorothy Dix.'

Adela bristled.

'What do you mean, a good sign? It would be a disaster if she became entangled with a man like that. I am hoping she will marry Lord Topham. That is why I invited her here. He is one of the richest men in England.'

'So you told me.'

'I went to endless trouble to get him away from the Gloria Pirbrights, just so that Kay could meet him. Gloria was sticking to him like flypaper. I shall speak to Kay very seriously. I am not going to have any nonsense.'

'Why don't you get Smedley to speak to her?'

'Smedley!'

'I always think a man can do these things so much more impressively. Women are apt to get shrill. And Smedley is the brother of the husband of the sister of Kay's father. Puts him almost *in loco Parentis*, you might say.'

Adela uttered a sound which in a woman of less impressive beauty would have been a snort.

'As if he could do anything. Smedley is a poor sheep who can't say boo to a goose.'

'Well, name three sheep who can.'

'Oh!'

'Yes?'

Adela was looking at Bill accusingly. Her manner was austere. In a hundred silent pictures she had looked just like that at a hundred heavies who had attempted in their uncouth way not to do right by our Nell. It was plain that some thought had floated into her mind which was reducing sisterly love to a minimum.

'Smedley!' she said. 'I knew there was something I wanted to ask you, but talking about Kay put it out of my head. Wilhelmina, have you been giving Smedley money?'

Bill had hoped that secrecy and silence might have been preserved on this point, but apparently it was not to be. She replied with as much nonchalance as she could manage on the spur of the moment.

'Why, yes, I did slip him a hundred dollars.'

'You idiot!'

'I'm sorry. I couldn't resist his pleading eye.'

'Well, you will be interested to hear that he was out all night on what I suppose was a drunken orgy. I went to his room after breakfast, and his bed had not been slept in. He must have sneaked off to Los Angeles with your precious hundred dollars.'

Bill did her best to soothe.

'Well, why agonize? He hasn't had a night out for years. Where's the harm in an occasional bender? Boys will be boys.'

'Smedley is not a boy.'

'What I always say is that as we shall pass this way only once, it surely behoves us – if behoves is the word I want – to do whatever in us lies to increase the sum of human happiness and—'

'Bah! Stuff and nonsense.'

'Yes, I suppose that is one way of looking at it.'

Adela went to the bell and pressed it.

'The only bright side of the thing,' she said, 'is that he will probably not return in time for lunch, and if he does, he will be in no condition to be at the table, to bore Mr Glutz with those interminable stories of his about Broadway in the 'thirties.'

'That's right,' said Bill. 'Always look for the silver lining. What are you ringing for?'

'I am expecting my masseuse. Oh, Phipps,' said Adela, as the door opened, 'has the masseuse arrived?'

'Yes, madam.'

'She is in my room?'

'Yes, madam.'

'Thank you,' said Adela coldly. 'Oh, Phipps.'

'Madam?'

Adela's face, which had hardened as she spoke of Smedley, grew harder.

'I wanted to see you, Phipps, to give you a piece of news which I think will be of interest to you.'

'Yes, madam?'

'You're fired!' said Adela, allowing the stormy emotion of which she had been Empress to leap from her eyes and scorch the butler like a jet from a flame thrower.

CHAPTER 5

Butlers, as the chronicler has already had occasion to remark in his observations on these fauna, are trained to hide their emotions. Whatever the turmoil in their souls, outwardly they aim at the easy insouciance of the Red Indian at the stake, and it is consequently not often that anyone is privileged to see one of them look aghast. But Phipps was now looking definitely aghast. His jaw had fallen and his eyes were round and horror-stricken.

He cast a tortured glance at Bill. 'Have you betrayed your promise?' the glance said. Bill's eye met his. 'Good heavens, no,' said Bill's eye. 'I haven't said a word. This is something completely new, and nobody more surprised than the undersigned.' Adela, having exploded her bomb, continued to ferment in silence.

'Fired, madam?' faltered Phipps.

'That's what I said.'

'But, madam—'

Bill intervened in her robust way. As Roget would have put it in his *Thesaurus*, she was surprised, astonished, perplexed, bewildered and at a loss, but she was not the woman to accept this sort of thing with meek detachment. She liked Phipps and wished him well, and he had told her that he particularly desired to remain in Adela's employment. Why this should be so, she could not imagine, but if that was how he felt, this totally unexpected thunderbolt must have been devastating. He was probably, she reflected with a pang, experiencing much the same sense of having been hit over the head with a blunt instrument as had come to her the previous afternoon on learning from Joe Davenport that his entire capital consisted of a few dollars and eight thousand tins of mixed soups.

'What do you mean, Adela? You can't fire *Phipps.*'

One would have said a moment before that it would have been impossible for even an Empress of Stormy Emotion to look sterner and haughtier than Adela Cork was looking. But at these words the proud severity of her manner took on a still more repellent coldness.

'Can't I?' she said crisply. 'Watch me.'

Bill became vehement. There were moments – this was one of them – when she had a nostalgic yearning to be back in the days of their mutual nursery, to return to the golden age when, if Adela annoyed her, she had been in a position to put a worm down the back of her neck or to smite her shrewdly with one of those hard objects which lie about nursery floors.

'You're crazy. You're like the base Indian who threw a pearl away richer than all his tribe. I haven't been long in this joint, but I've been here quite long enough to have got Phipps taped as the Butler Supreme.'

'Thank you, madam.'

'He's terrific. He out-Arthurs Treacher. He lends lustre to the whole establishment. That harsh, grating sound you hear from time to time is the envious gnashing of the teeth of all the other Beverly Hills employers who haven't got him. Fire him? Absurd. What on earth put a silly idea like that into your head?'

Adela continued stony.

'Have you quite finished?'

'No. But go on.'

'I am firing Phipps for a very good reason. Wouldn't you fire a butler who spends his whole time sneaking around in your bedroom?'

'Doing *what*?'

'That's what Phipps does. A couple of days ago I found him in my room, routing about in one of the closets. He said he had seen a spider.'

'Madam—'

Adela silenced the wretched man with an imperious gesture. She went on speaking in a voice that rose and vibrated with stormy passion.

'Yesterday he was there again. He said he had seen a mouse. As if there was the slightest possibility that there could be mice and spiders in my bedroom. And if it had been brimming over with mice and spiders, what business was that of his? I told him that if he ever put his ugly nose in my room again, I'd fire him. And this morning, as I was leaving for Pasadena, I went back to get a handkerchief, and there he was, if you please, under the dressing-table, with his fanny sticking up like a mesa in the Mojave desert. You leave at the end of the week, Phipps. I trust,' concluded Adela, her hand on the door handle, 'that I am a broad-minded woman, but I'm not going to share my bedroom with the butler.'

The sound of a door vigorously slammed died slowly away, leaving silence behind it. Bill was endeavouring to adjust her faculties to these sensational happenings. Phipps was standing rooted to the spot to which he had been rooted since his late employer's opening remarks, still exhibiting all the symptoms of having received a powerful blow in the solar plexus.

'For heaven's sake, Phipps, what's all this?' said Bill.

The butler came slowly to life, like a male Galatea. His face was pale and drawn.

'Would you object if I took a sip of your whisky and soda, madam?' he said in a low voice. 'I do not often indulge, but this has come as a shock.'

'Help yourself.'

'Thank you, madam.'

'And now,' said Bill, 'supply a few footnotes.' There was something of severity in her manner as she eyed the butler. 'Does this mean that you have been going back to your old activities? I thought you told me you had put all that sort of thing behind you.'

'Oh, no, madam, nothing like that.'

'Then what were you doing, routing about in cupboards and crawling under dressing-tables?'

'I – er – I was looking for something, madam.'

'I gathered that. But what?'

Once again the butler directed that searching glance at her. And, as before, the scrutiny apparently proved satisfactory. After the briefest of pauses, he replied, speaking in the hushed voice of the man who knows that walls have ears.

'The diary of the late Miss Flores, madam.'

'Good God!' said Bill. 'Isn't this where I came in?'

Phipps, having decided to be confidential, was now in the mind to hold nothing back.

'It was a remark of Mr Smedley's that gave me the idea, madam. Mr Smedley chanced to observe one night at dinner that it was highly probable that the late Miss Flores had kept a diary and that, in the event of her having done so, the volume was presumably somewhere on the premises. I was handing the potatoes at the moment, and the dish literally trembled in my grasp, madam. For the thought occurred to me immediately that the sort of diary kept by the sort of lady the late Miss Flores was would be worth a great deal of money to whoever found it.'

Bill eyed him gravely.

'Have you ever had that odd feeling, when somebody tells you something, Phipps, that you've heard it all before somewhere? Like hearing the familiar strains of some grand old anthem to which you have listened in childhood?'

'No, madam.'

'It happens sometimes. Well, go on.'

'Thank you, madam. I was saying that such a diary would be extremely valuable. The late Miss Flores, madam, was hot stuff, if I may venture to use the expression. In one quarter or another there would be a ready market for any diary which she had kept.'

'True. So you looked for it?'

'Yes, madam.'

'But didn't find it?'

'No, madam.'

'Too bad.'

'Yes, madam. Thinking the matter over, I reached the conclusion that, if the late Miss Flores had kept a diary, she would have secreted it somewhere in her sleeping apartment, the room now occupied by Mrs Cork.'

'So you said to yourself, "Yoicks! Tally ho!"?'

'Not precisely that, madam, but I proceeded to institute a diligent search, confident that I would eventually succeed in discovering its whereabouts.'

'That was why you were so anxious not to lose your job here?'

'Precisely, madam. And now I am leaving at the end of the

week. It is very bitter, madam,' said Phipps with a sigh that seemed to come up from the soles of his shapely feet.

Bill reflected.

'You've still got a couple of days.'

'But Mrs Cork will be on the alert, madam. I really could not go through the ordeal of being caught by her again.'

'Was she emotional?'

'Yes, madam. It was like being apprehended by a tigress while in the act of abstracting one of its cubs, madam.'

Bill shrugged her shoulders.

'Well, my heart bleeds for you, but I don't know what to advise.'

'No, madam.'

'It's a problem.'

'Yes, madam.'

'You might—'

Bill broke off. She had been about to suggest that the butler might slip into Adela's bedtime Ovaltine what is known as a knockout drop or Mickey Finn. She had one in her possession, the gift of a Third Avenue bartender with whom she was on cordial terms, and would have been delighted to lend it to him. But at this moment Kay came in through the french window, a bag of golf clubs over her shoulder, and the conference had to be suspended.

'Hi, Bill,' said Kay.

'Good morning, my child.'

'Good morning, Phipps.'

'Good morning, miss.'

Rosy with exercise, tanned by the Californian sun, Kay presented an attractive picture. Bill, looking at her, could follow

Joe Davenport's thought processes and understand his habit of proposing to her every hour on the hour.

'You two look very serious,' said Kay. 'What goes on?'

'Phipps and I were discussing the situation in China,' said Bill. 'He has been holding me spellbound.'

'Well, don't let me stop you.'

'Quite all right. Some other time, eh, Phipps?'

'Any time that suits you, madam.'

Kay threw her bag of clubs into a corner.

'Well, Bill. Working away?'

'Like a beaver.'

'On the *Memoirs*?'

'On the *Memoirs*.'

'Are they interesting?'

'Not in the least. I never realized before what dull lives silent screen stars led. It's agony, debasing my God-given talents with such hack-work.'

'It's a shame they let you go from the studio.'

'The loss is theirs. I've just got an idea for the finest B picture ever screened, and Superba-Llewellyn could have had it if they had not madly dispensed with my services. I shall write it up for *Horror Stories*. It's about a sinister scientist who gets hold of a girl and starts trying to turn her into a lobster.'

'A lobster?'

'You know. Those things that look like studio executives. He collected a covey of lobsters and mashed them up and extracted the juice, and he was just going to inject the brew into the gal's spinal column with a hypodermic syringe when her betrothed rushed in and stopped him.'

'Why did he do that?'

'He didn't want the girl he loved to be turned into something that looked like a studio executive. Isn't that good psychology?'

'I mean why did the sinister scientist act that way?'

'Oh, just a whim. You know what these sinister scientists are.'

'Well, it sounds fine. Full of meat.'

'Full of lobsters. Were you ever turned into a lobster, Phipps?'

'No, madam.'

'You're sure? Think back.'

'No, madam. I have not had that experience.'

'Well, go and ask the cook if she ever was.'

'Very good, madam,' said the butler courteously, and left the room. He had resumed his professional mask, and not even Sherlock Holmes, looking at his impassive face, could have guessed what vultures were gnawing at the bosom beneath that form-fitting shirt.

'Why all this research?' asked Kay.

'I'm a conscientious artist. I like to get my stuff right. If I'm doing a gangster story, I get it vetted by a gangster. If it's a hydrogen bomb story, I consult the firm that makes hydrogen bombs. And so on.'

'Yours must be very interesting work, Miss Shannon.'

'Well, it has brought me into contact with a lot of interesting people. I suppose I know more yeggs and thugs and crooks socially than anyone else in the United States. They send me cards at Christmas.'

'You're a disreputable old bird, aren't you, Bill. I wonder Aunt Adela has you in the house.'

'I'm doing those *Memoirs* of hers cheap. She never could resist a bargain. And don't use that expression "old bird". Hoity-toity, what next? However, as a matter of fact, the real reason why

I sent Phipps away to chat with the cook was that I wanted to take his mind off his troubles. Adela has just fired him.'

'Fired Phipps? Why?'

'It's a long story, too long to tell now. We'll go into it later. How was your golf game?'

'Weak and sinful. Lord Topham trimmed me. He broke a hundred.'

'Yes, he has just been releasing the story.'

'So you've seen him? Where is he?'

'Still at the telephone, I imagine. He went off to put in a trans-atlantic call about it at Adela's expense to a friend of his in London called Bingo or Stingo or something. And, while on the subject of telephones, Adela informs me that your young man called up yesterday. She wants to discuss it with you.'

'What young man?'

'Have you a dozen? Joe Davenport. Adela intercepted a pro-posal of marriage from Joe to you yesterday, and you wouldn't be far out in saying that she is exercised in her mind. She's hoping you'll marry that pleasant but quarter-witted ornament of the British peerage, Lord Topham.'

'Really? I suppose that's why she invited me here.'

'She specifically told me so.'

'Well, of course, it would be wonderful to be the wife of a man who can break a hundred. On the other hand—'

'Exactly. On the other hand. Don't overlook the fact that if you marry Topham, you'll have half a dozen imbecile children saying "Absolutely, what?" all the time in an Oxford accent.'

'Really, Miss Shannon!'

'Just a sneak preview.'

Phipps appeared.

'The cook desires me to say that she has never been turned into a lobster, madam.'

'We must face it like men, Phipps. Stiff upper lip, eh?'

'Yes, madam. I wonder if you could inform me of Mrs Cork's whereabouts, madam?'

'I imagine she's in her room. You know that room of hers. She was going to have a massage, if you remember.'

'Ah, yes, madam.'

'Do you want to see her?'

'Yes, madam.'

'I wouldn't at the moment.'

'No, madam.'

'What was it you wanted to see her about?'

'I wished to notify Mrs Cork that a Mr Davenport has arrived, madam.'

Kay uttered a cry.

'What?'

'Yes, miss. He is in the garage, putting his car away. His suitcases are in the hall.'

'His *suitcases*?'

'Yes, miss. I gathered from the gentleman that he passed the evening with Mr Smedley last night and Mr Smedley invited him to spend a few weeks with us. Thank you, miss.'

Phipps bowed slightly, and withdrew.

CHAPTER 6

Bill was the first to break the silence which followed his departure.

'Well, well,' said Bill.

Kay did not speak. She was feeling a little breathless. Phipps's announcement had given her the curious illusion of being the heroine of one of the silent films popularized by her Aunt Adela, in which the great feature had always been the pursuit of virtue by something pretty tough in the way of male pursuers. She had known that Joe was a pertinacious young man, but she had never suspected that his pertinacity would have carried him to such lengths as this. Even the most licentious of clubmen or the most bearded of desperadoes might well have hesitated to bring himself and suitcases into the home of Mrs Albert Cork on the invitation of her impecunious brother-in-law.

'Well, well,' said Bill. 'The soul of hospitality, Smedley. You would think he was a Southerner.'

'He must be crazy,' said Kay. 'He can't invite people here. This isn't his house.'

'As Adela will no doubt point out to him.'

Another facet of the mystery engaged Kay's attention.

'And what did Phipps mean, he passed the evening with Joe? Uncle Smedley never goes out. He told me so.'

'He did last night. He was on a toot.'

'So that's why he wasn't at dinner. I thought he had a headache.'

'He probably has.'

Kay was agitated. She was very fond of her Uncle Smedley, and the thought of what lay before him as the result of his thoughtless bonhomie touched her gentle heart.

'Do you think Aunt Adela will give him the devil?'

'If you want to bet against it, five will get you ten. But let's not discuss Smedley,' said Bill. 'Let us rather turn to the sacred meeting due to take place in a moment or two. So we are to have your young man with us for a few weeks, are we? Well, well, well.'

Kay had flushed. This may have been because Bill, her motion-picture training having taught her that a scene always goes better to a musical accompaniment, had begun to hum Mendelssohn's 'Wedding March', putting a good deal of feeling into it.

'Don't call him my young man. And it's more likely to be for a few minutes.'

'Do you think Adela will throw him out?'

'Don't you?'

'No. Not after I have pleaded his cause. I shall use all my eloquence on his behalf. We alumni of Superba-Llewellyn must stick together.'

Phipps appeared in the doorway.

'Mr Davenport,' he announced, and Joe came in, bringing, in Bill's opinion, the sunshine with him. Though suffering from the slight headache inevitable on the morning after an evening passed in the society of Smedley Cork when that earnest reveller was making up leeway after five years of abstinence, he was plainly in radiant spirits. He beamed on Bill and Kay, particularly the latter, with an almost Tophamic exuberance.

'Hello, there,' he said, and would no doubt, like Lord Topham, have added that this was the maddest, merriest day of all the glad new year, if he had happened to think of it. 'Hello, Bill.'

'Hello, Joe.'

'And, as I live and breathe, if it isn't my favourite glamour girl, Kay. Hello, Kay.'

'Good morning.'

'Well, here I am. Where's my hostess?'

'Having a massage. Well, Joe, if I'd known you were coming, I'd have baked a cake. You could have knocked me down with a feather when Phipps told us you were to be today's big surprise for my sister Adela.'

'Today's unpleasant surprise,' said Kay.

Joe looked hurt. The wrong note, he seemed to be saying, the wrong note entirely. On this morning of mornings he wanted there to be smiling faces about him. And nobody, not even a reasonably modest young man, likes to be told that his arrival is going to cast a blight on the home.

'Is it my imagination,' he said plaintively, 'or am I getting a rather tepid reception? I haven't got leprosy, you know.'

'You might just as well have,' said Kay.

'You don't think Mrs Cork will be pleased to see me?'

'You'll be lucky if you escape with a few flesh wounds. I warned you, you remember, that day at lunch.'

Bill intervened. She, too, thought the conversation was taking too morbid a tone.

'Nonsense,' she said. 'You may expect a warm Southern Californian welcome from Adela. Wait till I have reasoned with her.'

'Can anyone reason with Aunt Adela?'

'I can. I will play on her as on a stringed instrument. Don't you worry, Joe. I guarantee you will be treated as a ewe lamb. So you ran into our Smedley last night?'

'Yes.'

'An odd coincidence.'

'Not so very. I was outside the gate here in a taxi, and he came along and we fraternized.'

'What were you doing outside the gate in a taxi?'

'Just gazing. I gave him a lift down the hill. And when we found that he was at a loose end and I was at a loose end, it seemed the sensible thing to join forces. We started off with a bite at Mike Romanoff's.'

'And then?'

'We looked in at Mocambo. He began to unbend rather at Mocambo.'

'I can imagine.'

'After that we went on to Ciro's.'

'Where he unbent still further?'

'A good deal further.'

'That was when he invited you to come and stay here?'

'Yes.'

Bill nodded.

'I think I can reconstruct the scene. First, he climbed on the table and took his coat off and announced that he could lick any two men in the room.'

'Any three.'

'Then his mood seemed to soften. He climbed down, put his coat on, cried a little and invited everybody present to come and stay at his mountain home. "Particularly you, my dear fellow," he said to you.'

'You might have been there.'

'A pity I wasn't. What happened after that?'

'Well, all of a sudden I lost him. One moment he was there, the next he wasn't. Did you ever see the Indian Rope Trick?'

'No, but I know what you mean. He vanished?'

'Like a pea from under the shell. I don't know where he went.'

'Probably to one or more of the numerous joints on Ventura Boulevard. I know Smedley on these occasions. Eye-witnesses have informed me of his habits. He likes to get about and see fresh faces. The faces are always nice and fresh along the Ventura Boulevard, and no doubt he felt that he would be able to express and fulfil himself better if he were alone. I think, Kay, it might be as well if you whistled up the bloodhounds and started a search, to see if he got home all right.'

'I think it might.'

'We know that his bed was not slept in.'

'What!'

'So Adela says. She inspected it after breakfast. He was out all night.'

'Why does he do these things?'

Bill could answer that.

'Because he's a fathead. I have watched Smedley Cork burgeon from boyhood to man's estate. As a boy, he was a small fathead. He is now a large fathead. Tell me more,' said Bill, as Kay hurried out. 'Did Smedley do his imitation of Beatrice Lillie?'

'No, I don't remember that.'

'He usually does on these occasions, I'm told. First, his imitation of Beatrice Lillie, then in response to gales of applause, "Gunga Din" by the late Rudyard Kipling. It's terrific, I believe. How did you pass the long hours?'

Joe's face, which had become a little grave as the result of the introduction of the Mrs Cork motif, cleared. He began to beam again.

'Bill,' he said, 'I have tidings of great joy. You remember those characters who brought the good news from Aix to Ghent? Well, they weren't in my class, simply not in my class. I have good news that is good news. This is where you leap about and clap your little hands, my Wilhelmina. You ask me how we passed the long hours. Well, as soon as I thought the time was ripe, I started talking business.'

Bill's eyebrows rose.

'Business? With Smedley?'

'Selling him our authors' representatives scheme. It wasn't easy going, because his attention seemed to wander a good deal. I would put the thing with crystal clarity, and he would just sit back, looking glassy-eyed, like a fish on a slab, and when I said: "Well, how about it?" he was rather apt to spring to his feet and utter what I imagine were college yells of some prehistoric vintage. Putting the question aside, if you know what I mean. Which, of course, rendered it difficult for me to make a convincing sales talk. But I persevered, I kept at it, and you will be relieved to hear, pardner, that all is well. Snatching at a moment when he was having a comparatively lucid interval, I drove the thing home, and he's going to put up that twenty thousand we require as the first step up the ladder of wealth. For heaven's sake, woman,' said Joe, amazed, 'why aren't you leaping about and clapping your little hands? Haven't you been listening? Pop Cork has definitely promised to put up that twenty thousand we need to buy the agency.'

A sad, pitying look had come into Bill's face, the look of a mother forced to notify a loved child that his chances of obtaining candy are but slim, if not non-existent.

'There is a snag,' she said.

'Eh? What snag?'

'The fact that Smedley hasn't a cent in the world.'

'What!'

'Not a cent.'

Joe stared. He could make nothing of this.

'But you told me he was a millionaire.'

'Never.'

'You did. At the hotel yesterday. You said your sister married a millionaire.'

Bill's sad, pitying look deepened.

'Smedley isn't Adela's husband, my poor misled young friend. Adela's husband is no longer with us. Up there,' said Bill, pointing heavenwards. 'The gentleman with the harp. Smedley is merely his brother, and, as I say, he hasn't a cent in the world. For I hardly suppose that after such a majestic bender as he appears to have been on last night, he has anything left of the hundred I slipped him yesterday.'

Joe was rocking on his base.

'You mean that last night he was just kidding me?'

'I don't think intentionally.'

'Purely accidental, eh?'

Bill sighed. She was feeling like a mother who, in addition to having to notify him that there is no candy, has been compelled to strike a loved child on the base of the skull with a stocking full of sand.

'It's like this, Joe. When under the influence, poor Smedley gets delusions of grandeur. He believes he's back in the days when he really did have a lot of money ... before he fooled it all away on musicals which closed on Saturday and repertory companies nobody bought tickets for and Czechoslovak ballets and seasons of grand opera in English. He was at one time Broadway's leading angel. I suppose he backed more flops than any other two men in the business. Whenever there was anything more than ordinarily hopeless in the way of a dramatic opus knocking around, the cry immediately went up: "Where's Smedley?" It couldn't last. Five years ago his last few thousands went into a sweet little whimsical comedy adapted from the French which ran from a Friday night till the end of the week, and since then he has been penniless and dependent for his three squares a day on the grudging bounty of my sister Adela.'

She paused, and Joe, who had been clutching at the desk, slowly relaxed his grip.

'I see,' he said.

'I'm afraid this is something of a blow.'

'It is, rather. Yes, quite a disappointment. I believe I'll take a turn in the garden and brood on it a little.'

'I wish I could have broken it more gently.'

'Oh, that's all right,' said Joe dully.

He passed through the french window with bowed head, and Adela, appearing simultaneously in the doorway, gazed after him in surprise.

'Who is that?' she asked.

'Eh?' said Bill absently. Her thoughts were still occupied with Joe and the collapse of his hopes and dreams.

'That strange young man who just went out.'

Bill braced herself for combat.

'The young man to whom you allude,' she said, 'is not in the least strange. He is a perfectly normal, wholesome young man of the type which has made America what it is. That is Joe Davenport. You remember we were speaking of him not long ago.'

Adela reeled.

'Davenport! That man. What is he doing here? Did you invite him?'

'Not I. Smedley.'

Adela's beautiful eyes were bulging. She looked like Louise de Querouaille on one of her bad mornings. If some former associate of hers, with whom she had worked in the era when films were silent, had chanced to wander in at this moment and catch a glimpse of her face, he would have climbed the nearest jacaranda tree and pulled it up after him. Just so had she been wont to look in the old days when bursting in on a director in his office with the dreaded 'I should like a word with you, Mr Marsupial!' on her lips.

'Are you telling me that Smedley – *Smedley* – has been inviting people to my house?'

'That's right. It appears that they ran into one another last night and hobnobbed, and Smedley insisted on him coming to take pot luck for a week or two. You'll like Joe. One of the best.'

'Ha!'

Bill's manner became firm.

'Now listen, Adela,' she said. 'I had anticipated that you might be a little difficult about this, and I have formed my plans.'

'And I have formed mine. I shall order Phipps to throw this person out.'

'You will do no such thing. You will welcome him in and treat him like a ewe lamb. And when I say ewe lamb, I mean EWE LAMB. Adela, you and I were children together.'

'I have been trying to live it down ever since.'

'And when we were children together,' proceeded Bill, her voice cold and hard, 'I used, if you remember, to put worms down the back of your neck from time to time, when such a corrective to your insufferable behaviour seemed to be indicated. Persist in your refusal to become the genial hostess to my friend Joe Davenport, and I shall resume that practice.'

'We are not amused.'

'No, and you'll be still less amused after lunch when, as you show Jacob Glutz the rose garden, you find me sliding up behind you with a fistful of worms.'

Adela gasped. Forty years of acquaintance with her sister Wilhelmina had left her with the unpleasant feeling that she was not a woman to be trifled with. There might be things which her sister Wilhelmina would hesitate to do, but, she was forced to admit, not many.

'I believe you mean it!'

'Of course I mean it. Not one worm, mark you, but a bevy of worms. Large, fat, sticky worms, Adela. Slithery, writhing, wriggly worms. Cold, clammy—'

Adela capitulated.

'There is no necessity to labour your point,' she said stiffly.

'You see reason?'

'I am prepared to be civil to this friend of yours.'

'Good. Oh, Joe,' called Bill, going to the french window. 'Come here a minute, will you? Start practising that sunny smile of yours, Adela. I want to see it split your face from side to side. And when you address your guest, let your voice be like that of a turtle dove calling to its mate. Joe, I want you to meet your hostess. My sister, Mrs Cork.'

Joe's head was still bowed. Communing with nature, as represented by the orange trees, the lemon trees, the jacaranda trees and the rattlesnakes, had done little to alleviate the despondency which had him in its grip. Dully he was aware of something large and feminine confronting him, and he bowed in its direction.

'How do you do?' he said.

'How do you do?' said Adela with a visible effort.

'I have just been telling my sister that you are to be her house guest,' said Bill. 'She is overjoyed. Eh, Adela?'

There was a momentary silence.

'Yes,' said Adela.

'She says yes. So you may take up residence with an easy mind. Your status, as I foreshadowed, will be that of a ewe lamb.'

'Well, that's fine.'

'Yes, I think you will enjoy it. Ewe lambs live the life of Reilly. Ah, Lord Topham,' said Bill, as that gentleman entered with a brief What ho. 'Come and shake hands with Joe Davenport.'

'Hullo,' said Lord Topham, doing so.

'Hello,' said Joe.

'Hullo-ullo-ullo.'

'Yes,' said Joe.

There was another momentary silence.

'Perhaps you would show Mr Davenport his room, Lord Topham,' said Adela, seeming to speak with difficulty. 'It is the one next to yours.'

'Right ho,' said Lord Topham, for the task was well within his scope. He led Joe out. Through the open door he could be heard starting to describe to this new friend of his how he had broken a hundred this morning.

Bill sighed the contented sigh of the woman who has got things done.

'Well, Adela,' she said, 'I really must congratulate you. You were superb. Just the right note of warm but ladylike ecstasy. You might have been the Queen of Sheba welcoming King Solomon. But why do you look like that? Is there something on your mind?'

A wistful expression had come into Adela's face.

'I was only thinking,' she said, 'that a dozen times since you have been in this house I could have dropped something heavy on your head from an upper landing – and I didn't do it.'

'Of all sad words of tongue and pen, the saddest are these: It might have been. Well, Kay? What luck?'

Kay had come in, looking worried.

'I can't find him anywhere. Good morning, Aunt Adela. I've been trying to find Uncle Smedley.'

A whistling sound, like escaping steam, came from Adela's nostrils.

'I want to find Smedley myself,' she said grimly. 'I want to ask him what he means by inviting his revolting friends to my house.'

Bill seemed surprised.

'Why, I thought you liked Joe. You were charming to him just now. Perhaps Phipps can help us,' she said, as the butler came in bearing cocktail materials on a tray. 'Phipps, have you seen Mr Smedley?'

'Not since last night, madam.'

'You don't know where he is?' said Kay.

'Oh, yes, miss,' said the butler brightly. 'He is in prison.'

It was not immediately that any of those present found them-selves able to comment on this front page piece of news. Speech was wiped from their lips, and nothing left to them but the lan-guage of the eye, which is always unsatisfactory. Then Kay spoke.

'*Prison?*'

'Yes, miss. Mr Smedley is in the hands of the constabulary. He spoke to me on the telephone from the jail this morning.'

A shuddering cry broke from Adela's lips. Totting up the household expenses week by week and watching him at meals having twice of everything, she had sometimes – for she was a dreamer – aren't we all? – thought how nice it would be if her brother-in-law were a disembodied spirit, his mortal remains safely tucked away in the family vault, but she had never hoped that he would some day go to prison. Prison leads to publicity of the wrong sort, not only for the captive himself but for his rela-tives by marriage: KIN OF ADELA SHANNON JAILED, INSET-PHOTOGRAPH OF ADELA SHANNON. Adela Shannon was feeling, and the picture thus conjured up gave her an unpleasant, fluttering sensation internally, as if she had been swallowing butterflies.

'Oh, Lord!' she said.

'He suggested that I should come and take the requisite steps through the proper channels,' proceeded Phipps. 'But I was unable to leave my domestic duties.'

'It didn't occur to you to mention this to anyone?' said Bill.

'No, madam. Mr Smedley asked me to respect his confidence.'

Adela was clenching and unclenching her hands, going through the movements as if she were gripping a brother-in-law's throat. The thought may have been passing through her mind that in omitting to throttle Smedley earlier she had been remiss. One keeps putting these things off and is sorry later.

'Did you learn any details?' asked Bill.

'Yes, madam. Mr Smedley supplied me with the facts. While visiting a night club on the Ventura Boulevard last night, he stabbed the master of ceremonies with an oyster fork. The latter, visibly taken aback, summoned the management, who summoned the police, who removed Mr Smedley to the station house. I hope it will not get into the papers, madam.'

'I, too, Phipps. At the thought of what Louella Parsons would do with this the imagination boggles.'

'Yes, madam. It boggles perceptibly.'

'Phipps,' said Adela in a strangled voice, 'you may go.'

'Very good, madam.'

Relieved of the butler's presence, Adela was able to give full expression to the emotions surging within her. For some moments, she proceeded to speak of her brother-in-law in terms which could scarcely have been more severe if he had been a fiend with hatchet who had just slain six. It was almost a perfect character sketch of the absent man, and might have continued indefinitely had she not run out of breath. Bill, listening, was aware of an unwilling respect for a woman she had never liked. Adela, she felt, might have her faults, but you had to admire her vocabulary.

'Take it easy,' she urged.

'Take it easy? Ha! So this is what happens when I stop watching Smedley for a single instant. He's incorrigible.'

'A word I'll bet he couldn't have said last night.'

Phipps appeared.

'I thought you would wish to know, madam,' he said in a discreet, hushed voice, 'that Mr Smedley has just returned. He was entering the front door as I passed through the hall.'

'He's not in prison?' said Kay.

'Apparently not, miss.'

'How was he looking?'

'Not very roguish, miss.'

Adela's eyes flashed fire. Indeed, there was a sort of incandescence about her whole person. A bystander, had one been present, would have felt that if he had slapped her on the back, he would have burned his hand. Not that any bystander, unless exceptionally reckless, would have ventured to slap her on the back.

'Where is he?'

'He has gone to his room, madam, to shave.'

'And have a bath, no doubt,' said Bill.

'He has had a bath, madam. He was washed by the authorities.'

'Phipps,' said Adela, 'you may GO.'

'Very good, madam.'

'You'd better run up and view the body, Kay,' said Bill. 'He'll be wanting someone to hold his hand.'

Kay was looking apprehensively at Adela, who was staring before her with quivering nostrils.

'Bill, do do something. She's working herself up.'

'So I noticed,' said Bill. 'In moments of emotion, Adela always resembles those priests of Baal who gashed themselves with knives. But leave it to me. I'll attend to her.'

'What a comfort you are, Bill.'

'The Old Reliable.'

'Bless you.'

Kay hurried out, and Bill came back to Adela, who was now grinding her teeth.

'Now then, Adela,' she said briskly, 'simmer down. Come off the boil, will you please.'

'Don't talk to me!'

'That's just what I'm going to do. Adela, you make me sick.'

'Well, really!'

Bill, veteran of a hundred sisterly battles stretching back into the misty past of a mutual nursery, allowed her voice to rise. It was on these occasions that she was grateful to Providence for having equipped her with sound, healthy vocal cords. A situation like this could not have been handled adequately by a woman missing on one lung.

'Sick,' she repeated. 'Sitting there licking your lips at the prospect of tearing the stuffing out of poor old Smedley. What an infernal tyrant you are. You love harrying and torturing people. You're like Simon Legree, though you lack Simon's Legree's charm of manner. I always maintain that you killed old Al Cork.'

Adela, who had been about to take up the Simon Legree issue, decided to dispose of this charge first.

'My husband was run over by a sightseeing omnibus.'

Bill nodded. There was, of course, something in what she said.

'That may have helped,' she agreed, 'but it was being married to you that really did it. But it's silly having these family fights,' she went on, in milder vein. 'I'm sorry if I was rude.'

'You're always rude.'

'Well, ruder than usual. But I'm fond of Smedley. I was fond of him when he was a boy of fifteen with pimples. I was fond of him in his middle period, when he was scattering his money on Broadway turkeys. And I'm fond of him now. Some sort of mental flaw in me, I guess. Maybe I ought to see a psychiatrist. Still, there it is. So won't you skip the red tape and treat him decently?'

Adela bridled.

'I was under the impression that I had "treated him decently". I have supported him for five years. And a great strain it has been.'

'Strain be damned!'

'Must you curse and swear?'

'Of course I must. What do you expect me to do when you insult my intelligence by trying to put gobbledy-gook like that over on me? Strain, indeed! You could afford to support a dozen Smedleys. Al Cork left you enough money to sink a ship, not to mention specific instructions that you'd *got* to support Smedley. And whatever you spend on the poor devil, you get back in the gratification it affords your sadistic instincts to have him under your fat thumb. Am I being rude again?'

'You are.'

'I thought I was. All right, let's let it go. But don't forget about the quality of mercy. It isn't strained, you know. No, sir! It droppeth as the gentle rain upon the place beneath. So they tell me.'

'Quality of mercy? Stuff and nonsense.'

'You'd better not let Shakespeare hear you saying that.'

'I—'

Adela broke off, and stiffened. Her aspect had become that of a leopardess sighting its prey. Smedley was entering the room, followed by Kay.

'Ah!' she said.

Smedley, normally so dapper, was looking soiled and crumpled, like a Roman Emperor who has sat up too late over the Falernian wine. With the best intentions in the world, police officials, hustling a man out of a night club into the wagon and subsequently thrusting him into a cell, tend to spoil his crease. Smedley's Palm Beach suit looked as if it had been slept in, as indeed it had. But, oddly for a man with a criminal record and the appearance of a tramp cyclist, he was not slinking into the room with a shamefaced slouch, but striding in boldly in quite a dominant manner. His chin was up – both his chins were up – and in his bloodshot eye there gleamed defiance. It was as though from some inner source he had obtained courage and resolution.

Adela flexed her muscles.

'Well, Smedley?' she said.

'Well?' said Smedley.

'You rather had her there,' said Bill.

Smedley blinked. He peered as if he found some difficulty in focusing his gaze.

'Why, hello, Bill.'

'Hello, my old stag at eve.'

'I didn't see you. For some reason my eyes aren't at their best this morning. Floating spots. You look very yellow.'

'It's your imagination. I'm really a pretty pink.'

Adela, who had seated herself at the desk, rapped it imperiously. One felt that she would have preferred to have had a gavel, but, like Phipps when operating on a safe, she could do a lot with her finger tips.

'Never mind how Wilhelmina looks,' she said. 'I am waiting for an explanation.'

Bill raised her eyebrows.

'You feel that a man needs to explain why he stabbed a night club master of ceremonies? Just doin' what comes naturally, I'd say. But I should like to know why you aren't in prison, Smedley. Phipps gave us to understand that you were in a dungeon with dripping walls, being gnawed by rats. What happened? Did the jailer's daughter smuggle you in a file in a meat pie?'

'The judge let me off with a caution.'

'You see,' said Bill triumphantly. 'The quality of mercy *isn't* strained. Perhaps you'll believe me another time.'

Adela uttered a stricken moan, a moan of a good woman calling on heaven to witness her wrongs. Her voice shook and quivered as it would unquestionably have shaken and quivered in the days of her screen triumphs, had not her deeper emotions in that backward age had to be expressed in sub-titles.

'The shame of it!' she cried. 'The brother-in-law of Adela Shannon thrown into prison with all the riff-raff of Los Angeles!'

Kay caught Bill's eye.

'I suppose the society *is* a bit mixed in those prisons,' she said.

'Everything very informal, I believe,' said Bill.

'Does one dress?'

'Just a black tie.'

'PLEASE!!!' said Adela.

She turned to the prisoner again.

'Well, Smedley? I am still waiting for an explanation.'

'Tell her it's a poor heart that never rejoices.'

'Wilhelmina, please!'

'Well, it is,' said Bill. 'Ask anyone.'

'Have you an explanation?'

A curious writhing movement of the upper part of his body seemed to suggest that Smedley was trying to square his shoulders.

'Certainly I have an explanation. A complete and satisfactory explanation. I was celebrating.'

'Celebrating? Celebrating what?'

'The most amazing piece of good fortune that ever happened to a deserving man. I was telling Kay about it upstairs.'

Kay nodded.

'It's a real romance,' she said. 'It would make a good B picture.'

Bill frowned.

'Don't mention B pictures in my presence, girl. Would you twist the knife in the wound?'

'Oh, Bill, forgive me.'

'Quite all right, my child. You did but speak thoughtlessly. Tell us more, Smedley.'

Smedley swelled impressively. It was his moment. He was a man who as a rule found difficulty in getting himself listened to in the home circle. He had a fund of good stories, but Adela had a way of cutting them short in the opening stanzas. This was the first time in something like five years that he had actually been encouraged to hold the floor.

'Well, sir,' he said, 'it's like Kay was saying. It's a real romance. Yesterday evening I was out on the terrace, thinking of this and that, and suddenly my guardian angel whispered in my ear—'

'Oh, go and lie down,' said Adela wearily.

Smedley gave her a haughty look.

'I will not go and lie down.'

'No,' said Kay. 'I think you ought to hear about his guardian angel.'

'I am always glad to hear about guardian angels, always,' said Bill. 'What did yours whisper in your ear?'

'It whispered "Smedley, my boy, try the top of the wardrobe."'

Adela closed her eyes. She may have been praying, but more probably not.

'I really cannot endure this much longer.'

'I, on the other hand,' said Bill, 'could listen for ever. Proceed, Smedley. What wardrobe?' Where?'

'The one in Adela's bedroom.'

Adela started convulsively. Nor can she fairly be blamed for doing so. She was wondering if a woman's personal sleeping quarters had ever been so extensively invaded. First Phipps, and now Smedley. Was her bedroom her bedroom, she was asking herself, or was it the Grand Concourse of the New York Central Railroad terminal?

She shot a basilisk glare at the speaker.

'Have you been messing about in my room?'

'I went in there for a moment, yes. There was something I was trying to find.'

Sudden enlightenment came upon Bill.

'Ye gods!' she said. 'The diary?'

'Yup.'

'You were after that?'

'Yup.'

'Was it there?'

'Yup. Yessir, plumb spang on top of the wardrobe.'

'You've got it?'

'In my pocket,' said Smedley, patting it.

Adela was looking from Bill to Smedley, from Smedley to Bill, dangerously, exasperated by the mystic turn the conversation had taken. She disliked people who spoke in riddles in her presence, particularly if one of them was a jail bird who had brought disgrace on her home and the other a sister whom she wished she had never allowed to come into it. There were probably no two individuals in America who could have occasioned her more irritation by wrapping their meaning up in cryptic speech. Her resemblance to a peevish leopardess became more marked.

'What are you talking about? What diary? Whose diary?'

'Carmen Flores's,' said Kay. 'Uncle Smedley's been trying to find it for weeks.'

Bill sighed. Hers was a feeling heart.

'Alas, poor Phipps,' she said. 'What made you think of the wardrobe, Smedley?'

'If a woman has anything to hide, that's where she puts it. Well-known fact. It's in all the detective stories.'

'Don't you ever read Agatha Christie?' said Kay.

'Who is Agatha Christie?' asked Adela.

'My dear Adela!' said Bill.

Smedley gave a short, unpleasant laugh.

'Just a dumb bunny,' he said.

Adela drew herself up and directed at her brother-in-law a look of the sort which Evil Eye Fleagle of Brooklyn would have described as a full whammy.

'Don't you call me a dumb bunny, you – you fugitive from a chain gang!'

Smedley, in his turn, drew himself up.

'And don't you call me a fugitive from a chain gang. The idea!'

'I called you a fugitive from a chain gang because that's what you are. Don't the police want you?'

'No; the police do not want me.'

'How I sympathize with the police,' sighed Adela. 'I know just how they feel.'

Smedley stiffened.

'Adela, I resent that crack.'

'It doesn't matter what you resent.'

'Oh, doesn't it?'

'I think it does, Adela,' said Bill. 'This has put Smedley in a very different position from what he was this time yesterday.'

'I don't know what you mean.'

'It's very simple.'

Joe came in. He had seen his room, heard in pitiless detail the story of how Lord Topham had broken a hundred that morning, and he was now planning to go out into the garden and commune with nature again, not that he expected to derive any solace from doing so. He was still in the depths. Listlessly, he observed that the Garden Room seemed to have become the centre of a conference, but he paid its occupants but slight attention and was making for the french window, when Bill's powerful voice halted him in his tracks.

'Yesterday, Smedley was not in possession of the diary of the late Carmen Flores. Today he is. There isn't a studio in Hollywood that won't pay through the nose for it.'

Smedley corroborated this.

'I was on the phone to Colossal-Exquisite last night. They say they'll give fifty thousand.'

'Fifty thousand!' gasped Adela.

'Fifty thousand,' said Smedley.

Adela rose slowly to her feet.

'You mean that they ... You mean fifty thousand *dollars*?'

'Fifty thousand dollars,' said Smedley.

Joe tottered to the sofa, and collapsed on it. His head was spinning. It seemed to him that an unseen orchestra had begun to play soft music in the Garden Room.

'Have you closed with the offer?' asked Bill.

'No. I'm waiting till all the bids are in. I'm expecting big things from Medulla-Oblongata-Glutz.'

'But you can't get less than fifty thousand.'

'That's right,' said Smedley. He took the diary from his pocket, and gazed at it reverently. 'Isn't it astounding that a small book like this should be worth fifty grand!'

'It must be red-hot stuff. Have you read any of it?'

'I can't. It's in Spanish.'

'Too bad.'

'Quite all right,' said Smedley, quick to point out the bright side. 'One of the gardeners at the Lulabelle Mahaffy place down the road is a Mexican. I'm going to take it around to him and have him translate it. We're good friends. He gave me a shot of that Mexican drink once that they call – no, I've forgotten the name, but it lifts the top of your head off.'

On Adela during these exchanges there had descended a curious calm. It was as if she had been thinking and had been rewarded with an idea whose effects had been to still the tumult within her. Her fingers were twitching a little, but her voice, when she spoke, was quiet and unusually amiable.

'I picked up a little Spanish when I made that personal good-will tour in South America,' she said. 'I might be able to help you. May I look?'

'Sure,' said Smedley cordially. Speak civilly to Smedley Cork and he would speak civilly to you. 'There's an entry for the twenty-first of April that I'd like to have translated. It's got six exclamation marks against it in the margin.'

He gave Adela the book. Her fingers, as she took it, were twitching more noticeably than ever. She started for the door, and Smedley, suddenly filled with a nameless fear, gave tongue.

'Hey! Where are you off to?'

Adela turned.

'A thing as valuable as this ought not to be left lying about. I will put it in the safe in the projection room.'

'You will not. I want it on my person.'

Adela unmasked her batteries.

'Well, you aren't going to have it on your person,' she said crisply. 'For five years, Smedley, you have been living on me, and it is high time you made some contribution to the household expenses. This is it.'

'But – but—'

'This is it,' said Adela. 'Fifty thousand dollars. A very nice first instalment. And, Wilhelmina,' she said, changing the subject, 'will you kindly go and take off those damned dungarees. You look like a rag-picker.'

The slam of the closing door was drowned by the cry, resembling in its general features the howl of some bereaved beast of the jungle, which broke from Smedley's lips. Phipps, in his remarks to Bill on the previous day with reference to the attitude of Mrs Adela Cork toward those whom she found exploring her bedroom, had spoken of the emotional behaviour of tigresses when robbed of their cubs. It is to be doubted whether even the most neurotic tigress could have put more naked anguish into what in motion picture circles is called a 'take' than Smedley was now doing. His eyes seemed to protrude from their sockets, and a third chin had been added to his normal two by the limp sagging of his jaw.

Bill, also, appeared a little taken aback by this unforeseen development.

'Hell!' said Bill. 'Hijacked!'

Smedley had joined Joe on the sofa.

'In broad daylight!' he moaned incredulously. His bosom swelled with righteous indignation. 'I'll – I'll write to the *Los Angeles Examiner*.'

'No wonder that woman rose to impressive heights on the silent screen.'

'But she can't do this,' cried Joe.

'I know she can't,' said Bill. 'But she has.'

She crossed the room with a firm step and touched the bell. She was a woman of action, not one of your weak, fluttering women who waste precious time in lamentations. It had taken her scarcely a moment to see what Napoleon would have done in a crisis like this. Put Napoleon in a tight corner, and the first thing he did was summon up his reserves and send them into battle.

This was what Bill now proposed to do. The ringing of that bell was the bugle call which would bring Phipps hurrying to the front line, and it was on Phipps that she was relying to snatch victory out of defeat. If something valuable has been wrested from you and deposited in a safe and you have at your call a butler who has taken twenty lessons in the art of opening safes and become good at it, it is mere common sense to avail yourself of his skill.

Smedley was still vibrating. He raised his hands in a passionate gesture.

'I'll write to *Variety*!'

Bill regarded him maternally.

'Pipe down, Smedley.'

'I won't pipe down. I'll write to Walter Winchell.'

'No need to get excited,' said Bill. 'Absolutely not, as Lord Topham would say. Ah, Phipps.'

The butler had manifested himself silently in the doorway.

'You rang, madam?'

'Yes. Come in. Phipps,' said Bill, 'I'm afraid the moment has arrived when we must cease to hide your light beneath a bushel.'

'Madam?'

'Smedley, have you ever served on a jury?'

As far as an English butler can quiver, Phipps quivered. He gave Bill a startled look.

'Madam, please!'

Bill ignored the interruption.

'I was on one some little time ago,' she said. 'The one that sent Phipps here up the river for three years.'

'Madam, you promised—'

'And do you know what he had done to earn that three years' sojourn in the coop? Do you know what he got his scholarship at Sing-Sing for? Safeblowing.'

If she had anticipated a stunned reaction to her words, she was not disappointed. Smedley stopped blowing invisible bubbles and stared dumbly at the butler. Kay gave a sharp squeak and stared dumbly at the butler. Joe said 'What?' He, too, stared dumbly at the butler. Phipps stared dumbly at Bill. Not even Julius Cæsar, receiving Brutus's dagger thrust, could have packed more pain and disappointment into a glance. Those reproachful eyes made Bill feel that something in the nature of an apology was in order.

'I'm sorry, Phipps,' she said, 'but this is a military necessity.'

Smedley found speech.

'You mean,' he said, marvelling, 'that Phipps – *Phipps* – was a safeblower?'

'And a darned good one, too. He blew a beautiful safe.'

'Then—'

'Exactly. That is why I brought up the subject. Phipps, we've got a job for you.'

Though far from having recovered completely from one of the worst shocks of his life, the butler was sufficiently himself again to be able to speak.

'Madam?'

'We want you to open Mrs Cork's safe. The one in the projection room.'

'But, madam, I have retired.'

'Then this is where you make a comeback.'

Icy resolution descended upon Phipps. It was those operative words 'Mrs Cork's safe' that steeled him to resist to the uttermost this call upon his services. As Lyly so neatly put it in his *Euphues*, the burned child dreadeth the fire, and a butler who has twice been caught by Mrs Cork hunting for diaries in her bedroom does not lightly undertake the even more perilous task of burgling safes belonging to a woman of her intimidating personality. Call on James Phipps to make a burglarious entry into Fort Knox and it is possible that he might decide to oblige, but Mrs Cork's safes were immune.

'No, madam,' he said respectfully, but firmly.

'Ah, come on.'

'No, madam.'

'Think well, Phipps. Are you prepared to stand before the bar of world opinion as a man who refused to bust a safe to oblige an old friend?'

'Yes, madam.'

'I should have mentioned at the outset,' said Bill, 'that your cut will be five thousand dollars.'

Phipps started. His iron front began to waver. His eyes, which had been hard and uncompromising, softened, and there came into them the gleam which always comes into the eyes of butlers when they see an opportunity of making quick money. The vision of Adela Cork sneaking up behind him and tapping him on the shoulder as he crouched before her safe began to fade. Every man has his price, and five thousand dollars was about Phipps's.

'That is a lot of money, madam,' he said, impressed.

'It's a hell of a lot of money,' said Smedley, thoroughly concurring.

Bill checked this parsimonious trend of thought with an impatient gesture. How like Smedley, she felt, to haggle at a time like this.

'Customary agent's commission of ten per cent,' she said. 'We mustn't be tightwads. You don't want Phipps to think he's working for Gaspard the Miser. Five thousand of the best, Phipps.'

'Five thousand,' murmured the butler reverently.

'Are you with us?'

'Yes, madam.'

A general sense of relaxation came over those present, such as occurs at a theatrical conference when the man with the money has been induced to sign on the dotted line.

'Good,' said Bill. 'Well, here's the story outline. Last night, Mr Smedley found the diary.'

'Oh, my Gawd!'

Bill patted his shoulder tenderly.

'I know, I know. I know just how you feel. But there it is. Mr Smedley found the diary last night, and this morning Mrs Cork swiped it from him and put it in the safe in the projection room. Will you reswipe it for us?'

That vision of Adela creeping up behind him flashed once more before the butler's eyes. A momentary shudder, and he was strong again.

'For five thousand dollars, yes, madam.'

'Fine. Then we will meet at Philippi – or, rather, here – tonight. Say at one o'clock in the morning.'

'One o'clock in the morning. Very good, madam. Will that be all, madam?'

'That will be all.'

'Thank you, madam.'

'Thank *you*, Phipps.'

'Bill,' cried Smedley, 'you're a marvel. What a brain, what a brain!'

'Wonderful,' said Kay. 'Stupendous.'

'Colossal,' said Joe.

'Super-colossal,' said Smedley.

'You can always trust me, boys,' said Bill. 'The Old Reliable.'

Adela came in. She was wearing the contented look of a woman who has just locked the door of her personal safe on a diary valued at a minimum of fifty thousand dollars. Then her eyes flashed with all their old fire.

'Wilhelmina!' she cried. 'Those dungarees! Are you aware that Mr Glutz's car is coming up the drive?'

'Sorry,' said Bill. 'I was thinking of other things. I will rush up immediately and gown myself in some clinging material which will accentuate rather than hide my graceful outlines.'

'Well, be quick.'

'Forked lightning, my dear Adela, forked lightning.'

Smedley Cork, first of the little group of Phipps's admirers and supporters to arrive at the tryst, stood at the open french window of the Garden Room, staring into the night with unseeing eyes. From somewhere outside the closed door there came the *ping* of a clock striking one, and he heard it with a feeling of amazement. Only one o'clock? He could scarcely believe it. For though in actual fact not more than five minutes had elapsed since he had crept furtively down the stairs and come to the meeting place, it seemed to him that he had been waiting there for weeks. He was faintly surprised that he had not put out tendrils, like a Virginia creeper.

Strained nerves play these tricks on us, and Smedley's nerves were strained at the moment to their uttermost. Reason told him that it was improbable that his sister-in-law, a woman who was fond of her sleep, would take it into her head to roam the house at this hour, but the hideous possibility of such a disaster had not failed to present itself to his shrinking mind, and the native hue of resolution on his face was sicklied o'er with the pale cast of thought. As he stood there waiting for zero hour, his substantial frame twitched and quivered and rippled, as if he had been an Ouled Nail dancer about to go into her muscle dance.

The door opened noiselessly, and Bill came in. She was in her customary excellent spirits. Others might view with concern the shape of things to come, but not Wilhelmina Shannon. She was looking forward with bright enthusiasm to a pleasant and instructive evening.

'Hello, there, Smedley,' she boomed in her breezy, genial way, and Smedley leaped like an Ouled Nail dancer who has trodden on a tin-tack.

'I wish you wouldn't bellow at a fellow suddenly like that, Bill,' he said aggrievedly, having descended to terra firma. He was panting heavily and not feeling at all easy about his blood pressure. 'If anyone had told me that an old friend like you would come and sneak up behind a man at a time like this and yell in his ear without the slightest preliminary warning, I wouldn't have believed it.'

'Sorry, old sport.'

'Too late to be sorry now,' said Smedley moodily. 'You made me bite my tongue off at the roots. Where's Phipps?'

'He'll be here.'

'It's past one.'

'Only just,' said Bill. She joined him at the window and gazed out on the night. 'What were you doing? Admiring the stars? A fine display. Glorious technicolour. Look how the floor of heaven is thick inlaid with patines of bright gold. In such a night as this, when the sweet wind did gently kiss the trees—'

'For God's sake, Bill!'

'Some other time, eh? Not in the mood, no? Just as you say. Still, you can't deny that yonder stars are well worth looking at. Bright, twinkling and extremely neatly arranged. A credit to Southern California. I'll tell you something about those stars, Smedley. There's not the smallest orb which thou beholdest, but in his motion like an angel sings, still quiring to the young-eyed

Cherubim. Worth knowing, that. Stop fluttering like a butterfly in a storm. What's the matter with you? Nervous?'

'I'm all of a twitter.'

'Too bad. Ah, Joe,' said Bill, as the door opened again. 'Come in and help me hold Smedley's hand. He's got the heeby-jeebies.'

Joe regarded the sufferer with a sympathetic eye. He, too, was by no means free from that distressing malady. He was conscious of an unpleasant sensation of having been plunged into the middle of a B picture of the more violent type and this was making him gulp a good deal. His had been a sheltered life, and it is disconcerting for a young man who has lived a sheltered life, to find himself involved in happenings of a melodramatic nature. To him, as to Smedley, there had come the thought that they might at any moment be joined by his formidable hostess, and it was not an agreeable reflection. Estimating Mrs Cork's probable reactions to the discovery that her nearest and dearest were planning to burgle her safe, his imagination boggled – as Phipps would have said, perceptibly. He had conceived a wholesome awe of the ex-Empress of Stormy Emotions. Running over in his mind the women of his acquaintance who could legitimately be classed as dangerous specimens whose bite spelled death, he was inclined to place Adela Shannon Cork at the very top of the list. She had that certain something that the others had not got.

'Where's Phipps?' he asked, having swallowed a little painfully, for something – possibly his heart – seemed to be obstructing his throat.

'He's coming,' said Bill. 'The hour will produce the man.'

Smedley whinnied like a frightened horse.

'But it hasn't produced the man, damn it. Here it is past one and not a sign of him. You keep saying he's coming, but he doesn't come. I'm going up to his room, to see if he's there. I shall probably find him curled up in bed, fast asleep. Curse the fellow. Letting us down like this. If that's the sort of butler England is turning out nowadays, I'm sorry for them.'

He hurried from the room, puffing emotionally, and Bill clicked her tongue disapprovingly, like a Spartan mother who had expected better things of a favourite son.

'Smedley gets so agitated.'

'I don't blame him,' said Joe. 'I'm agitated myself.'

Bill snorted scornfully.

'You men! Just neurotic wrecks, all of you. No sang-froid.'

'All right, I lack sang-froid and I'm a neurotic wreck. But I repeat that I am agitated. That's my story and I stick to it. My feet are chilly, and there's something with long hairy legs running up and down my spine. Suppose this ghastly butler doesn't show up.'

'He'll show up.'

'Well, suppose he can't open the safe?'

To Bill, who with eleven other good men and women true had sat for several days in a jury box while the absent man's capabilities were expatiated on by an eloquent District Attorney, who made a capital story out of it, the question was a laughable one.

'Of course he can open the safe. He's an expert. You should have read what the papers said of him at the time of the trial. He got rave notices.'

Joe became calmer.

'He did?'

'He certainly did.'

'He has your confidence?'

'Implicit.'

Joe expelled a deep breath.

'Bill, you put heart into me.'

'That's good.'

'I suppose it's because one doesn't associate a butler with safe-blowing that I was doubtful for a moment. I always thought butlers went about saying "Yes, m'lord", "No, m'lord", "Pardon me, m'lady, Her Grace the Duchess is on the telephone. She desires me to ask if you can spare her a cup of sugar", and all that sort of thing, not blowing safes. But if he carries your guarantee, that's a different matter. I feel now that prosperity is just around the corner.'

'Let's sing to every citizen and for'gner prosperity is just around the corner.'

'Yes, let's. Bill, you know all about women, I take it?'

'I've met a couple.'

'Women like money. Right?'

'Right.'

'And they like a man who does things. A man, I mean, who is what the French call an *om sayrioo*. Correct?'

'Correct.'

'So if Phipps gets that diary and Smedley gives us our twenty thousand and I become a plutocratic partner in a flourishing firm of authors' representatives, it's going to make a whale of a lot of difference, don't you think? With Kay, I mean. She'll feel a new respect for me.'

'She will probably throw herself on your chest and cry "My hero!"'

'Exactly. Something more or less along those lines is what I'm budgeting for. But we need Phipps.'

'We do.'

'Without Phipps we can accomplish nothing constructive.'

'Nothing.'

'Then what it all boils down to is, Where the hell is Phipps?

Ah!' said Joe, breaking off and uttering the ejaculation with satisfaction and relief. The door was opening again.

It was, however, not the missing man, but Kay who came in. She was looking charming in pyjamas, mules and a dressing-gown, and at any other time Joe's heart would have leaped up like that of the poet Wordsworth when he, the poet Words-worth, beheld a rainbow in the sky. Now he merely stared at her bleakly, as if by failing to be a butler with a gift for blowing safes she had disappointed him.

'You!' he said.

'Come aboard, sir,' said Kay. 'Where's Phipps?'

Bill's manner, too, was austere.

'Now don't you begin,' she said, 'I thought I told you to go to bed.'

'Please, sergeant, I got up.'

'Well, you're a naughty girl and will probably come to a bad end, but now you're here, you can make yourself useful. You can be cutting sandwiches.'

'You can't want sandwiches after that enormous dinner.'

'I always want sandwiches,' said Bill. Her momentary annoy-ance had vanished. She scrutinized Kay critically.

'An attractive little cheesemite, isn't she, Joe? Get those eyes.'

'I've got 'em.'

'Thank you, Bill. I'm glad you think I have nice eyes.'

Joe could not pass this. The first agony of seeing somebody who was not Phipps coming in at the door had abated, and he was able to take in those pyjamas, that dressing-gown and the mules. The wistful thought came to him that, if he and Kay had a little home, this was how she would look in it of an evening.

'Nice!' he said. 'Good God! what an adjective!'

'What Joe means,' explained Bill, 'is that with your limited vocabulary you have failed to spike the *mot juste*. In analysing your appearance, he feels, we must not be satisfied with the first weak word that comes along. We must pull up our socks and dredge the Thesaurus. You probably consider, Joe, that those eyes of hers are more like twin stars than anything?'

'Twin stars is nearer it. You're on the right lines.'

'And her brow? Alabaster?'

'I'll accept alabaster.'

Kay took a seat, kicked off one of the mules and tried unsuccessfully to catch it on her toe. Like her Aunt Wilhelmina, she was in capital spirits and feeling none of the tremors which afflicted the more timorous males.

'If you two have quite finished discussing me—' she said.

'Finished?' said Bill. 'Why, we've scarcely begun. We've barely scratched the surface. I like her bone structure, Joe. She has small, delicate bones.'

Joe endorsed this.

'That was the first thing I noticed about her the day we met, her small, delicate bones. "Gosh!" I said to myself. "This girl's got small, delicate bones."'

'And what happened then?' asked Kay.

'His heart stood still,' said Bill. 'I should have mentioned that when Joe was a boy, he promised his mother he would never marry a girl who didn't have small, delicate bones. Well, Smedley? Did you find him curled up in bed?'

Smedley had come puffing in, more agitated than ever. It was plain that the mystery of the missing butler was preying heavily on what may loosely be called his mind.

'Not a sign of him. He's not in his room. What on earth can have happened to the fellow?' He broke off, leaping in the old familiar way, his eyes protruding from their sockets. 'What's that?'

'What's what?'

'I heard something. Outside there. Footsteps.'

'Be calm, Smedley,' said Bill. 'It's probably Phipps. I'll bet it's Phipps. I think it's Phipps. It *is* Phipps,' she concluded, as a dignified figure detached itself from the darkness outside the french windows. 'Good evening, Phipps.'

'Good evening, madam,' said the butler.

CHAPTER 10

With the arrival of the star performer, the spearhead of the movement and, if one may so describe him, the pilot on whom they were counting to weather the storm, a general feeling of relief and relaxation spread itself among the other members of the expeditionary force. Smedley grunted. So did Joe. Kay smiled a welcoming smile. And Bill, as if lost to all sense of what was fitting, went so far as to pat the man on the shoulder. Dressed in what appeared to be his Sunday best, his gaze calm and steady, he seemed so competent, so reliable, so obviously capable of conducting to a successful conclusion any task to which he set the hand holding the bowler hat without which no English butler stirs abroad.

'Well met by moonlight, proud Phipps,' said Bill. 'We thought you were never coming.'

'I am a little late, I fear, madam. I was detained. I am sorry.'

'Not at all. But I admit that we had begun to be somewhat anxious. Mr Smedley in particular had reached a condition where he could have given Mariana at the Moated Grange six bisques and a beating. What detained you?'

'I was in conference with Mr Glutz, madam.'

Smedley's eyes, which had returned to their sockets, popped out again.

'Mr who?'

'Glutz, sir. Of Medulla-Oblongata-Glutz. The gentleman who was with us for luncheon today. He sent for me to discuss details of my contract.'

'Your *what?*'

The butler placed his bowler hat on the desk, carefully and a little formally, like Royalty laying a foundation stone.

'My contract, sir. If I might explain. I had withdrawn to my pantry at the conclusion of the midday meal, and Mr Glutz presented himself there and after a few courteous preliminaries opened negotiations with a view to my playing butler roles in his organization.'

'Good God.'

'Yes, sir, I must confess to having experienced a slight feeling of surprise myself when I heard him formulate his proposition. Indeed, I fancied for a moment that this was a mere passing pleasantry on the gentleman's part – what is known in my native country as a bit of spoof and in the United States of Northern America as ribbing. But I soon perceived that he was in earnest. Apparently, he had been greatly impressed by my deportment at the luncheon table.'

'I don't wonder,' said Bill. 'You were right in mid-season form. It was buttling plus.'

'Thank you, madam. One desires to give satisfaction. Mr Glutz expressed much the same opinion. He appeared to feel that if talents like mine – artistry like mine, he was kind enough to say – were transferred to the silver screen, nothing but good could result. He then made me the offer to which I have referred, and I accepted it.'

He ceased, walked to the bowler hat, lovingly flicked a speck of dust off it, and returned to the statuesque pose which he was wont to assume at meal times, looking as if he were about to have his portrait painted by an artist who specialized in butlers. On his audience an awed silence had descended. It is always impressive to be present at the birth of a star.

'Well, well,' said Smedley.

'Fancy!' said Kay.

'So now you're in pix,' said Joe.

'Yes, sir.'

'Extraordinary how everybody in Hollywood wants to get into pix,' said Bill.

'Yes, madam. The aspiration would appear to be universal.'

Bill said it was something in the air, and Phipps said, So one would be disposed to imagine, madam, adding that oddly enough he had occasionally toyed with the idea of embarking on a motion-picture career, but had never seemed to find the time to get around to it: and the conversation might have continued in this purely professional vein, had not Smedley, recovering from his first reactions to the sensational news item, become peevish and fussy again.

'But why on earth had you got to see him at this time of night?' he demanded, not perhaps unreasonably. 'One o'clock in the morning!'

A well-trained butler's eyebrows never actually rise, but Phipps's flickered as if on the verge of upward movement, and in his voice, as he replied, there was the merest hint of rebuke.

'My domestic duties would not allow me to leave the house before eleven-thirty, sir, and Mr Glutz was insistent that the negotiations be completed without delay. I took the view that his wish was law.'

'Quite right,' said Bill. 'Always keep in with the boss, however much he looks like a lobster. Mr Glutz does look like a lobster, doesn't he?'

'There is perhaps a resemblance to the crustacean you mention, madam.'

'Though what does that matter, provided his heart is in the right place?'

'Precisely, madam.'

'People have told me I look like a German Boxer.'

'A most attractive Boxer, madam.'

'Nice of you to say so, Phipps. Has he given you a good contract?'

'Eminently satisfactory, thank you, madam.'

'Watch those options.'

'Yes, madam.'

'Well, I shall follow your future career with considerable interest.'

'Thank you, madam. I shall endeavour to give satisfaction.'

Smedley, who had a one-track mind, struck the practical note.

'Well, now you're here, let's get to work. We've wasted half the night.'

'It won't take long,' Bill assured him, 'if Phipps is the man he used to be. Eh, Phipps?'

The butler seemed to hesitate. He looked like a butler about to break bad news.

'I am sorry, madam,' he said apologetically, 'but I fear I have a slight disappointment for you.'

'Eh?'

'I have come to inform you – regretfully – that I am unable to undertake the desired task.'

If he had expected to make a sensation, he was not wrong. His words had the effect of a bombshell.

'What?' cried Joe.

'Oh, Phipps!' cried Kay.

'Not undertake it?' bleated Smedley. 'What do you mean?'

It was plain that the spearhead of the movement was embarrassed. He departed from his official impassivity to the extent of shuffling a foot along the carpet and twiddling his fingers. Then his eyes fell on the bowler hat, and he seemed to draw strength from it.

'This unforeseen development has naturally effected a considerable alteration in my plans, sir. As an artist in the employ of Medulla-Oblongata-Glutz, I cannot run the risk of being discovered burgling safes. There is a morality clause in my contract.'

'A *what*?'

'Morality clause, sir. Para Six.'

Smedley exploded. His blood pressure had now reached unprecedented heights. A doctor, scanning his empurpled face, would have clicked his tongue concernedly – or perhaps would have rubbed his hands, scenting business at ten dollars a visit.

'I never heard such infernal nonsense in my life.'

'I am sorry, sir. But I fear I cannot recede from my position.'

'But think of that five thousand.'

'A trivial sum, sir. We motion-picture actors regard five thousand dollars as the merest small change.'

'Don't talk like that,' cried Smedley, shocked to the core. 'It – it's blasphemous.'

Phipps turned to Bill, in whom he seemed to see a level-headed ally and supporter.

'I am sure *you* will understand that I cannot jeopardize my contract, madam.'

'Of course not. Your art comes first.'

'Precisely, madam.'

'You've signed on the dotted line, and you must stay signed.'

'Exactly, madam.'

'But, damn it—'

'Hush, Smedley. Be calm.'

'Calm!'

'What you need,' said Bill, 'is a drink. Could you bring us a few fluid ounces of the blushful Hippocrene, Phipps?'

'Certainly, madam. What would you desire?'

Smedley sank into a chair.

'Bring every darned bottle you can lay your hands on!'

'Very good, sir,' said Phipps.

He retrieved the bowler hat from the desk, seemed for an instant about to place it on his head, recollected himself in time and left the room on his errand of mercy.

Silence reigned for some moments after his departure. Smedley in his chair was looking like a man who for two pins would have buried his face in his hands. Joe had gone to the french window and was staring up at the stars with a lack-lustre eye. Kay had crossed to where Smedley sat and was stroking his head in a rather feverish manner. Only Bill was unmoved.

'Well,' said Smedley, from the depths, 'this is a nice thing to happen.'

'Just Hollywood,' said Bill.

'If a man's a butler, why can't he *be* a butler, instead of gallivanting around getting contracts from studios? And all this nonsense about morality clauses.'

'Cheer up, Smedley. All is not lost. I have the situation well in hand,' said Bill. And such was the magnetism of her personality, that a faint hope stirred in Smedley's bosom. It might be, he felt, that even the present impasse would yield to treatment from one whom, though he did not want to marry her, he had always recognized as a woman of impressive gifts, well worthy of the title of The Old Reliable. He raised a haggard face.

'What are you going to do?'

'I am going to have a drink.'

Joe, at the window, barked bitterly like the seal to which Kay had once compared him.

'Fine,' he said. 'Splendid. You're going to have a drink, are you? That has taken a great weight off my mind. I was worrying myself sick, wondering if you were going to have a drink.'

'And having had it,' proceeded Bill equably, 'I shall press one on Phipps. When he comes back, I propose to ply him with strong liquor and – after his calm judgment has been sufficiently unbalanced – taunt him.'

'Taunt him?'

'What do you mean, taunt him?' asked Smedley, puzzled but still hopeful.

'Sting his professional pride with a few well-judged sneers. Scoff and mock at him for having lost his grip. It ought to work. Phipps, you must remember, till he saw the light, was a very eminent safeblower, and you can't be an eminent safeblower without being a sensitive artist, proud of your skill and resentful of criticism. Imagine how Shakespeare would have felt if, after he had retired to Stratford, somebody had come along and congratulated him on having got out of the theatre game just in time, because it was obvious to everyone that he had been slipping.'

The door opened, and Phipps came in, swaying slightly under the weight of an enormous tray filled with bottles and glasses. He placed it on the desk.

'I have made a wide selection, madam,' he said.

'You certainly have,' said Bill. 'Start pouring, Joe.'

'Right,' said Joe, becoming busy. 'Champagne, Bill?'

'Just a drop, perhaps. I often say that there's nothing like a little something at this time of night to pick you up. Thank you, Joe. But you haven't got yours, Phipps.'

'Nothing for me, thank you, madam.'

'Oh come. We must drink success to your new venture. You are embarking on a career which is going to make you loved, worshipped, idolized by the prince in his palace, the peasant in his cot, the explorer in the jungle and the Eskimo in his frozen igloo, and your launching must be celebrated with fitting rites. Properly speaking, we ought to break a bottle over your head.'

'Well, a very mild one, madam. I have always been somewhat susceptible to the effects of alcohol. It was that that led to me being on trial on the occasion when you were a member of the jury, madam.'

'Really?'

'Yes, madam. The constables would never have apprehended me if I had not been under the influence.'

'Of course, yes, I remember. It came out in the evidence, didn't it? Your employer heard noises in the night, tracked them down to the library, where his safe was, and there you were, lying back in a chair with your feet on the table and a bottle in your hand, singing "Sweet Adeline".'

'Precisely, madam. It rendered me conspicuous.'

During these exchanges, Bill, her massive form interposed between the butler and the desk, had been selecting with almost loving care one bottle after another and blending their contents in a large tumbler. It was liquid dynamite that she was concocting, but her words, as she handed him the mixture, were reassuring.

'Try this for size,' said Bill. 'I think you'll like it. I call it the

Wilhelmina Shannon Special. Mild – practically a soft drink – but refreshing.'

'Thank you, madam,' said Phipps, accepting the glass and raising it to his lips with a respectful 'Happy days, madam'. He sipped tentatively, then more deeply, finally drained the bumper with evident relish.

'How was it?' asked Bill.

'Extremely good, madam.'

'Will you have another one?'

'I believe I will, madam.'

Bill took the glass from him and put a second Wilhelmina Shannon Special in preparation.

'Tell me about yourself, Phipps,' she said, chatting as she mixed. 'Our paths parted after that trial. I, so to speak, took the high road, and you took the low road. Let us pick up the threads. What happened after you graduated from Sing-Sing?'

'I secured a position as a butler once more. Thank you, madam,' said Phipps, taking the glass.

'No difficulty about getting signed up?'

'Oh, no, madam. I had a number of excellent references from employers in England, and I came to California, affecting to be a newly arrived immigrant. Ladies and gentlemen in California rarely read the New York papers, I have found. And, after all, three years had passed since my unpleasant experience. I suffered no inconvenience whatsoever.'

'And how about the old life work?'

'Madam?'

'Did you continue to pass the potatoes with one hand and blow safes with the other?'

'Oh, no, madam.'

'Just buttled?'

'Precisely, madam.'

'So it's about four years since you did a job?'

'Yes, madam.'

'Then no wonder you've lost your nerve,' said Bill.

The butler started. A dull flush spread itself over his face, deepening the colour already implanted there by the Wilhelmina Shannon Specials.

'Madam?' he said.

Bill was friendly, but frank.

'Oh, you can't fool us, Phipps. That was a good story of yours about your morality clause, but we see through it.' She turned to Joe. 'Right?'

'Right,' said Joe.

'It's perfectly plain that after your long lay-off, you realized that you were no longer the man you had been. You had lost your grip, and you knew it.' She turned to Kay. 'Right?'

'Right,' said Kay.

'Listen,' said Phipps.

He spoke harshly and in a manner quite lacking in his customary smooth deference. His voice had taken on a novel roughness. His head, as he had said, had never been strong, and there had been that in the beverage assembled by his hostess which might have roughened the voice of a seasoned toper. It was as though the butler in him had fallen from him like a garment, revealing the natural man beneath. That his *amour-propre* had been deeply wounded was plainly to be seen.

'Oh, don't think we're blaming you,' said Bill. 'Some people might say you were a spineless poltroon—'

'*What?*'

'– but that's all nonsense. You aren't a poltroon, you're just prudent. You know when a thing is beyond your powers and you decline to take it on. We respect you for it. We applaud your good sense. We admire you enormously. Right?'

'Right,' said Joe.

Phipps scowled darkly. His eyes were hard and hostile.

'You think I'm scared to bust that pete upstairs?'

'It seems the reasonable explanation. And I don't wonder. It's a tough job.'

'Tough? A lousy little country house pete? Listen, I've busted banks.'

'You mean piggy banks?'

'No, I don't mean piggy banks. I'll show you,' said Phipps, and started for the door. 'I'll show you,' he repeated, his hand on the handle.

'But where are your tools?' bleated Smedley.

'He doesn't need tools,' said Bill. 'He does it all with his finger tips, like Jimmy Valentine. He is a most gifted artist – or, rather, was.'

'*Was?*' cried Phipps. He wrenched the door open. 'Come on. Let's go.'

'I'll come with you,' said Smedley, entranced.

'So will I,' said Joe. 'And in case you feel faint—'

He took up the tray and added himself to the procession. Bill closed the door behind them and came back to Kay, who was regarding her with the light of admiration and respect in her eyes. It was a light that often came into the eyes of those privileged to observe The Old Reliable when at her best.

'So that's that,' said Bill. 'Amazing what you can do with a little tact. And now that we are alone, my girl, sit down and listen to me, because I've a bone to pick with you. What's all this I hear about you and Joe?'

CHAPTER 11

Kay laughed.

'Oh, Joe!' she said.

An austere frown darkened Bill's brow. She disapproved of this spirit of levity. Ever a staunch friend, she had been much touched by Joe's story of his romance, with its modern avoidance of the happy ending. Feeling as she did about Smedley, she could understand and sympathize.

'Don't giggle in that obscene way,' she said sternly. 'He's a very fine young fellow, Joe Davenport, and he loves you.'

'So he keeps telling me.'

' "Bill," he said to me only the day before yesterday, and if there weren't tears in his eyes as he spoke, I don't know a tear in the eye when I see one, "Bill, old sport, I love that girl." And then a lot of stuff about depression and debility and night sweats and loss of appetite. And in addition to the tear in his eye, there was a choking sob in his voice, and he writhed like a dynamo. He worships you, that boy. He adores you. He would die for one little rose from your hair. And does he get one? Not so much as a blasted petal. Instead of thanking heaven, fasting, for a good man's love, you reply to his pleadings with the horse's laugh and slip him the brusheroo. Nice goings-on, I must say.'

Kay stooped over and kissed the top of Bill's head. She had

had a feeling that this was going to be good, and she saw that she had not been mistaken.

'You're very eloquent, Bill.'

'Of course I'm eloquent. I'm speaking from a full heart on top of three glasses of champagne. Why are you pulling this hard-to-get stuff on Joe? What's wrong with the poor fish?'

'He knows. I told him exactly why I wouldn't marry him, when we had lunch together the day before I left New York.'

'Aren't you going to marry him?'

'No.'

'You're crazy.'

'He's crazy.'

'About you.'

'About everything.'

'Why do you say that?'

'Well, isn't he?'

'Not in the least. A man I respect and admire. Don't you like him?'

'Yes. Very much. He's fun.'

'I'm glad you didn't say "He's a good sort."'

'Why, is that bad?'

'Fatal. It would have meant that there was no hope for him. It's what the boys used to say of me twenty years ago. "Oh, Bill," they'd say. "Dear old Bill. I like Bill. She's a good sort." And then they'd leave me flat on my keister and go off and buy candy and orchids for the other girls, blister their insides.'

'Is that why you're a solitary chip drifting down the river of life?'

'That's why. Often a bridesmaid but never a bride.'

'You poor old ruin.'

'Don't call me a poor old ruin. Does respect for an aunt mean nothing to you? And don't try to steer me off the subject of Joe. Fourteen times you've refused him, he tells me.'

'Fifteen. He proposed again in the rose garden this afternoon.'

Bill snorted indignantly. She rose and walked with measured step to the desk, intending to restore her composure with more champagne, found that the tray of drinks was no longer there, snorted again, this time with disappointment, sighed heavily and returned to her seat.

'Well, I don't understand you,' she said. 'I simply don't understand you. The workings of your mind are a sealed book to me. If I were a girl and Joe Davenport came along and wanted to marry me, I'd grapple him to my soul with hoops of steel. Gosh, when one looks around and sees what a jerk the average young man is, the idea of a girl with any sense in her head turning down a fellow like Joe is incredible.'

'He seems to have made a great impression on you.'

'He has. I regard him as a son.'

'Grandson.'

'I said *son*. Yes, I regard him as a son, and you know how I've always felt about you. You're as fresh as an April breeze, you get off impertinent cracks about grandsons, you mock at my grey hairs and will probably sooner or later bring them in sorrow to the grave, but I love you.'

'Mutual, Bill.'

'Don't interrupt. I say I love you. And I have your best interests at heart. I consider that this J. Davenport is the right man for you, and it is my dearest wish to park myself in a ringside pew and bellow "The Voice That Breathed O'er Eden" while you and he go centre-aisle-ing. It beats me why you aren't thinking along the same lines. It isn't as if you had anything against the poor simp. You admit you like him.'

'Of course I like him. How could anyone help liking Joe?'

'Then what's the trouble?'

Kay was silent for a moment. There had come into her face that grave, intent look which attracted Joe so much. With the toe of one of her mules, she traced an arabesque on the carpet.

'Shall I take my hair down, Bill?'

'Certainly. Tell me all.'

'Well, then, I could fall in love with Joe in a minute – like *that* – if I'd let myself.'

'And why don't you?'

Kay went to the french window and looked up at the stars.

'I'm – wary.'

'How do you mean, wary?'

'Well ... Bill, how do you look on marriage? I mean, is it a solemn, sacred what-d'you-call-it that's going to last the rest of your life – or a sort of comic weekend like some of these Hollywood things? I think it's pretty solemn and sacred, and that's where Joe and I seem to differ. No, don't interrupt, or I shall never be able to explain. What I'm really trying to say is that I can't bring myself to trust Joe. I can't believe he's sincere.'

With a powerful effort, Bill had managed to restrain herself from breaking in on what she considered the most absurd speech to which she had ever listened, and she was a woman who had sat in on a hundred studio conferences, but she could maintain silence no longer.

'Sincere? Joe? For heaven's sake! How often do you want him to ask you to marry him before it filters through into your fat little head that he's fond of you?'

'It isn't how often he asks me, it's how he asks me. He does it as if the whole thing were a tremendous joke. And I don't regard love as a joke. I'm stuffy and sentimental and take it seriously.

I want someone who takes it as seriously as I do, not someone who can't make love to a girl without making her feel as if she were the stooge in a vaudeville act. How does he expect me to feel,' said Kay, becoming vehement, for the grievance was one that had long been festering within her, 'when his idea of romantic wooing is to grin like a Cheshire cat and say "Don't look now, but will you marry me?" When a girl's with the man she loves, she doesn't want to feel as if she had been wrecked on a desert island with Groucho Marx.'

There was silence for a moment.

'Then – just between us girls – you do love Joe?'

'Of course I do,' said Kay. 'I've loved him right from the start. But I don't trust him.'

Silence fell again. Bill began to see that this was going to be difficult.

'I know what you mean,' she said at length. 'Joe *is* apt to clown. The light comedy manner. The kidding approach. But don't forget that clowning is often just a defensive armour against shyness.'

'You aren't trying to tell me that Joe's shy?'

'Of course he's shy – with you. Every man's shy when he's really in love. That's why he acts like that. He's like a small boy trying to ease the embarrassment of wooing the belle of the kindergarten by standing on his head. Don't you be deceived by the surface manner, my girl. Look past it to the palpitating heart within.'

'You think Joe has a palpitating heart?'

'You betcher.'

'So do I. I think it palpitates for every girl he meets who isn't an absolute gargoyle. I've seen his little red book.'

'His what?'

'Telephone numbers, Bill. Telephone numbers of blondes, brunettes, redheads and subsidiary blondes. Don't you understand the facts of life, my child? Joe is a butterfly, flitting from flower to flower and making love to every girl he meets.'

'Is that what butterflies do?'

'You can't stop 'em. He's another Dick Mills.'

'Another who?'

'A man I was once engaged to. We broke it off.'

'Was he a butterfly?'

'Yes, Bill, he was.'

'And you feel that Joe is like him?'

'The same type.'

'You're all wrong.'

'I don't think so.'

Bill swelled belligerently. Her blue eyes flashed fire. Though of a more equable temperament than her sister Adela and not so ready as that formidable woman to decline on all occasions to Stand Nonsense, she could be pushed just so far. Like Mr Churchill, there were things up with which she would not put.

'It doesn't matter what you think, my girl. Let me tell you something for your files. It is my unshakeable opinion that you and Joe were made for one another. I have studied you both with loving care, I am convinced that you would hit it off like ham and eggs, and I shall omit no word or act to promote the merger. I intend to bring you together, if it's the last thing I do. And you know me. The Old Reliable. And now go and cut those sandwiches. All this talking has made me hungry.'

As Kay started for the door, it opened and Smedley came in, startling both of them. In the pressure of other matters, they had quite forgotten Smedley.

Smedley was looking agitated.

'Where are you going?' he asked. 'Not up to the projection room?'

'She's going to the kitchen to cut sandwiches,' said Bill. 'I thought we needed a little sustenance, to keep the machine from breaking down.'

'I'm glad,' said Smedley, relieved. 'I wouldn't want you to go up there just now. Those drinks you gave Phipps, Bill, have had a curious effect on him. They seem to have – er – melted his reserve. He keeps stopping work to tell risky stories.'

'Dear, dear. Off colour?'

'Very. There was one about a strip-tease dancer and a performing flea ...' He looked at Kay, and paused. 'But it wouldn't interest you.'

'I've heard it,' said Kay, and went off to cut sandwiches.

Smedley mopped his forehead. His morale seemed to have hit a new low. The rush and swirl of the night's events had plainly left him weak. Marcus Aurelius, who held that nothing happens to anybody which he is not fitted by nature to bear, would have had a hard time selling that idea to Smedley Cork.

'I'm worried, Bill,' said Smedley.

'You're always worried.'

'Well, haven't I enough to worry me? When I think of what it means to me to have Phipps open that safe! And he won't concentrate. He lets his mind wander. He's displaying a frivolous side to his nature which I wouldn't have believed existed. Do you know that just before I left he was proposing to imitate four Hawaiians? The man's blotto.'

Bill nodded.

'I ought to be more careful with those Wilhelmina Shannon Specials,' she said. 'The trouble is, I don't know my own strength.'

'And it isn't only that he refuses to get down to his job. It's the noise he's making. Loud bursts of fiendish laughter. I'm so afraid he'll wake Adela.'

'Her room's on the other side of the house.'

'But even so.'

Bill shook her head.

'You know, looking back,' she said, 'where we made our big mistake was in not giving Adela a Mickey Finn. It would have —' She broke off. 'Good heavens!'

'What's the matter?'

Bill was feeling in the pocket of her slacks. When she brought her hand out, there was a small white pellet in it.

'This is a Mickey Finn,' she said. 'It was given me from his personal stockpile by a bartender on Third Avenue, a dear old friend of mine. He said it would be bound to come in handy one of these days, and how right he was. I had intended to slip it into Adela's bedtime Ovaltine, and I forgot.'

'And now too late.'

'And now too late,' said Bill. 'Too late, too—'

Her voice trailed away. From just outside the door there had come the sound of a loud and raucous laugh. She looked at Smedley, and he looked at her, with a wild surmise.

'Suffering cats!' said Smedley. 'That's Phipps.'

'Or could it have been a hyena?' said Bill.

It was Phipps. He came in, followed by Joe, laughing heartily like one of the Chorus of Villagers in an old-fashioned comic opera. Tray in hand, he selected a bottle, went to the sofa, seated himself on it and leaned back comfortably against the cushions. It was plain that for the time being, he had shelved all idea of work and was regarding this as a purely social occasion.

CHAPTER 12

'Good evening, all,' said Phipps genially, and refreshed himself from the bottle. Whatever prudent concern he might once have felt regarding his constitutional inability to absorb alcoholic stimulants in large quantities without paying the penalty had clearly vanished. Wine is a mocker and strong drink is raging, and he liked it that way. Any time wine wanted to mock him, his whole demeanour suggested, it was all right with James Phipps, and the same went for strong drink when it wished to rage. 'Good evening, all,' he said. 'I will now imitate four Hawaiians.'

His obvious eagerness to spare no effort to make the party go would have touched and delighted some such person as a fun-loving Babylonian monarch of the old school, always on the look-out for sympathetic fellow revellers to help the Babylonian orgy along, but to Smedley his words seemed to presage doom and disaster. What it was that four Hawaiians did when performing for the public entertainment, he did not know, but instinct told him that it was probably something pretty loud, and he quivered apprehensively. Adela's room might, as Bill had said, be on the other side of the house, but, as he had said to Bill, 'even so'.

'No, no!' he squeaked, like a mouse in pain.

'Then I'll sing "Sweet Adeline",' said Phipps with the air of a man who only strove to please. His repertory was wide, and if the audience did not want the four Hawaiians, 'Sweet Adeline' would do just as well.

This time it was Joe who lodged a protest. Joe was fully as agitated as Smedley. He was familiar with 'Sweet Adeline'. He had sung that popular song himself in clubhouse locker rooms, and none knew better than he that its melody contained certain barbershop chords which, dished out as this sozzled major-domo would dish them out, must inevitably penetrate bricks and mortar like butter, rousing a sleeping hostess from her slumbers as if the Last Trump had sounded. Once more there rose before his eyes the vision of Mrs Adela Shannon Cork sailing in through the door in a dressing-gown, and that thing with the long hairy legs went galloping up and down his spine again.

'No, please, Phipps,' he urged.

The butler stiffened. He was in genial, pleasure-seeking mood and all prepared to unbend with the boys, but even at the risk of spoiling the harmony he felt obliged to insist on the deference due to his position. Once allow the lower middle classes to become familiar, and where were you?

'Mister Phipps, if *you* please,' he said coldly.

Bill, always tactful, added her weight to the rebuke.

'Yes, be careful how you speak to Mr Phipps, Joe. You can see he's fractious. I think he's teething. But I wouldn't sing "Sweet Adeline", Mr Phipps.'

'Why wouldn't I sing Sweet "Adeline"?'

'You'll wake sweet Adela.'

'You mean Ma Cork?'

'Ma Cork is correct.'

Phipps mused. He took another sip from his bottle.

'Ma Cork,' he said meditatively. 'Now, there's a woman I never cared for. How would it be to go and give her a jolly good punch in the nose?'

It was a suggestion which at any other time would have enchanted Smedley, for if ever there was a woman who from early childhood had been asking, nay clamouring, for a good sock on the beezer, that woman in his opinion was his sister-in-law Adela. But now he shuddered from head to foot and uttered another of his mouselike squeaks.

'No, no!'

'Not give her a punch in the nose? Just as you say,' said Phipps agreeably. He could be as reasonable as the next man if you treated him with proper respect. 'Then let's have a gargle. Not you, Smedley,' he went on. 'You've had enough. The old coot's been mopping it up like a vacuum cleaner,' he explained amusedly. He surveyed the coot with an indulgent eye. 'Old drunken Smedley!' he said. 'Where were you last night, you old jail bird? Hey, Smedley?'

Smedley smiled a wry, preoccupied smile. Phipps, piqued, raised his voice a little.

'HEY, SMEDLEY!!'

Bill said 'Hush!' Joe said 'Hush!' Smedley leaped as if he had been unexpectedly bitten by a shark.

Phipps's sense of grievance deepened. It seemed to him that these people were deliberately going out of their way to ruffle him. When he said: 'Hey!' they said: 'Hush!', and as for the old lush Smedley, who was patently pie-eyed, he didn't so much as bother to answer when spoken to civilly. One would have to be pretty sharp, felt Phipps, on this sort of thing.

'Well, why doesn't he say Hey when I say Hey? When a gentleman says Hey to another gentleman, he expects the other gentleman to say Hey to him.'

Smedley was prompt to retrieve his social lapse.

'Hey,' he said hastily.

'Hey, what?'

'Hey, Mr Phipps.'

The butler frowned. His mood had now definitely darkened. Gone was that warmth of bonhomie and goodwill which had filled him when he came into the room, making him the little brother of all mankind and more like a walking sunbeam than anything. He found in Smedley's manner a formality and lack of chumminess of which he thoroughly disapproved. It was as though he had started hobnobbing with a Babylonian monarch and the Babylonian monarch had suddenly turned around and snubbed him, as Babylonian monarchs are so apt to do.

'Come, come,' he said. 'None of your standoffishness. Say Hey, Jimmy.'

'Hey, Jimmy.'

Phipps, a perfectionist, was not yet satisfied.

'Say it again, more loving like.'

'Hey, Jimmy.'

Phipps relaxed. Smedley's intonation had not been altogether that of a love bird passing a remark to another love bird, but it had been near enough to mollify him. Genuine feeling in it, it seemed to him.

'That's better. Can't have you sticking on dog just because you're a ruddy Society butterfly.'

'Don't you like ruddy Society butterflies?' asked Bill, interested.

Phipps shook his head austerely.

'No. Don't approve of 'em. Comes the Revolution, they'll be hanging on lamp posts. The whole system's wrong. Ain't I a man? ... AIN'T I, SMEDLEY?'

Smedley leaped.

'Yes, yes, of course you are, Jimmy.'

'Ain't I a gentleman?'

'Of course, Jimmy, of course.'

'Then fetch me a cushion for me head, you old souse. Come on, now. Hurry. I want a little service around here.'

Smedley brought the cushion and propped it behind his head.

'Comfortable – Jimmy?' he said, between his teeth.

The butler froze him with a glance.

'Who are you calling Jimmy? Address me as Mr Phipps.'

'I'm sorry, Mr Phipps.'

'And so you ought to be. I know your sort, know 'em well. Grinding the face of the poor and taking the bread out of the mouths of the widow and the orphan. Comes the Revolution, blood'll be running in streams down Park Avenue and Sutton Place'll be all cluttered up with corpses.'

Smedley drew Bill aside.

'If this is going to continue,' he muttered, 'I cannot answer for the consequences, Bill. My blood pressure is rising.'

'Comes the Revolution,' Bill reminded him, 'you won't have any blood. It'll be running down Park Avenue.'

'I'm going up to listen at Adela's door. Make sure she's asleep. Anything to get away for a moment from that sozzled son of a . . .' He caught Phipps's eye and broke off. He smiled a difficult smile. 'Hey, Mr Phipps!'

The butler's eye was too glazed for fire to flash from it, but his manner showed that he was offended.

'How many times have I got to tell you to call me Jimmy?'

'I'm sorry, Jimmy.'

'Mister Phipps, if you *don't* mind,' said the butler sternly.

Smedley, plainly unequal to the intellectual pressure of the conversation, gave it up and hurried out. Bill, glad to be relieved of his disturbing presence, struck the business note.

'Well, Mr Phipps,' she said, 'how's it coming? If you are feeling sufficiently rested, you might be having another go at that safe.'

'Yes,' agreed Joe. 'We mustn't waste any more time.'

He had said the wrong thing. The butler stiffened again. For some reason, possibly because of that earlier lapse into familiarity, he seemed to have taken a dislike to Joe. He gave him an unpleasant look.

'What's it got to do with *you*, may I ask?'

'Everything. You see, it's this way – Mr Smedley—'

'You mean old drunken Smedley?'

'That's right. Old drunken Smedley is in with Miss Shannon—'

'You mean old dogfaced Bill here?'

'That's right. Old drunken Smedley is in with old dogfaced Bill here and me on a business deal. He's putting up the money.'

'What money?'

'The money he'll get when he gets that diary.'

'What diary?'

'The diary in the safe.'

'What safe?' asked Phipps keenly, like a prosecuting attorney questioning some rat of the underworld as to where he was on the night of June the fifteenth.

Joe looked at Bill. Like Smedley, he found Phipps's conversational methods a little bewildering.

'The safe you're going to open, Mr Phipps.'

'Who says I'm going to open any safes?'

'I don't,' said Bill, taking charge in her competent way. 'You couldn't do it.'

'Do what?'

'Open that safe.'

Phipps was silent for a space, digesting this.

'You say I couldn't open that safe?'

'No. It's hopeless to think of attempting it. Four years ago you would have been able to, yes, but not now. We're all agreed on that.'

'On what?'

'That you were a good man once, but you've lost your nerve. We went into it all before, if you remember, and we came to the conclusion that you no longer had the stuff. You're finished.'

'Ho!'

'A pity, but there it is. Not your fault, of course, but you're a back number. As a safeblower, you're washed up. You buttle like nobody's business, you have a bright future on the silver screen, but – you – can't – open – the safe.'

Wine when it is red – or, as in the case of Phipps, who was drinking *crème de menthe*, green – stingeth like an adder, and so do adverse criticisms of his skill as an artist. Phipps was thus in the position of a man who is stung by two adders simultaneously, and his flushed face grew darker.

'Ho!' he said. 'Can't open the safe, eh? Can't open the ruddy safe? Well, just for that I *will* open the ruddy safe.'

Joe shot a quick, reverential look at Bill. Leave it to The Old Reliable, he was feeling. The Old Reliable would always see you through.

'Thank you, Phipps,' he said.

'Thank *you*, sir,' said the butler automatically. 'I mean,' he added quickly, correcting himself, 'what you thanking me for?'

'I told you. You say you're going to open the safe. Well, if you open the safe, we'll get our money.'

'Ho? And when you do, I suppose you think you're going to

marry that young Kay? What a hope. You haven't a chance, you poor fish. *I* heard her turning you down in the rose garden this afternoon.'

Joe started.

'What?'

'Like a bedspread.'

Joe blushed a pretty pink. He had not supposed that he had been playing to an audience.

'You weren't there?'

'Yes, I was.'

'I didn't see you.'

'Nobody don't ever see me.'

'They call him The Shadow,' said Bill.

'And I'll tell you what struck me about the episode,' proceeded Phipps, having looked once more upon the wine when it was green. 'Your methods are wrong. You're too light-hearted and humorous. You won't win the heart of a sensitive girl by cracking gags. What you want to do is to fold her in your arms and kiss her.'

'He daren't,' said Bill. 'It isn't safe. He once kissed a girl in Paris and she shot clear up to the top of the Eiffel Tower.'

'Ho?'

'Just closed her eyes with a little moan of ecstasy and floated up – and up – and up.'

To illustrate, Bill twiddled her fingers, and the butler stared at them austerely.

'Don't do that!' he said sharply. 'It makes me think of spiders.'

'I'm sorry. You dislike spiders?'

'Yes, I do. Spiders!' said Phipps darkly. 'I could tell you something about spiders. You ask me, if you want to hear all about spiders.'

'Comes the Revolution, spiders will be running down Park Avenue.'

'Ah,' said Phipps, as if conceding this as probably correct. He yawned, and swung his feet up on the sofa. 'Well, I don't know what you two are going to do,' he said. 'I'm going to get a little shut-eye. Good night, all. Time for Bedfordshire.'

His eyes closed. He gurgled a couple of times. Then, still clutching the bottle, he slept.

CHAPTER 13

Joe looked at Bill, dismayed. In this world one should be prepared for everything, or where is one, but he had not been
prepared for this. It had come on him as a complete surprise.

'Now what?' he said.

The new development appeared to have left Bill unconcerned.
She regarded the horizontal butler with something of the tender
affection of a mother bending over the cradle of her sleeping
child, and adjusted the pillow behind his head, which looked like
slipping.

'Probably all for the best,' she said. 'A little folding of the hands
in sleep will do him good, and we have the rest of the night to
operate in. Did you ever see a blotto butler before?'

'Never.'

'Nor I. In which connection, I would state that I'd rather see
than be one. When the cold grey light of the dawn comes stealing
in through yonder windows in an hour or so, you and I will be
in the pink and as fresh as daisies, but one shudders to think how
Jimmy Phipps will be feeling. On the morning after a binge like
that, the state of man, as Shakespeare says, suffers the nature of
an insurrection. There should be a big run on the bromo-seltzer
'ere long. But let's not wander from the point. Though brilliantly
lit and not always too coherent in his remarks, the recent pickled

herring said one very sensible and significant thing. About your methods of conducting your wooing. Were you listening?'

'I was.'

'He was right, you know. He touched the spot. Your methods *are* wrong. I've been talking to Kay. That girl loves you, Joe.'

'What?'

'She told me so in so many words. The way she actually phrased it has slipped my memory, but the gist of her remarks was that when in your presence she feels as though there was only a thin sheet of tissue paper between her and heaven. And if that isn't love, what is?'

Joe reeled.

'Bill, if you're kidding me—'

'Of course I'm not kidding you. What on earth would I want to kid you for? She loves you, I tell you. You're the cream in her coffee, you're the salt in her stew. But she's wary ... cagey ... She's suspicious of you.'

'Suspicious? Why?'

'Because you clown all the time.'

'I'm shy.'

'I told her that, but she didn't believe me. She looks on you as an insubstantial butterfly, flitting from flower to flower and sipping. Are you a sipper?'

'No, I'm not a sipper.'

'You don't play around with girls?'

'Certainly not.'

'Then how about your little red book of telephone numbers?' said Bill.

If she had slapped a wet towel across Joe's face, the effect could not have been more pronounced. When you slap a wet towel across a man's face, he gasps and totters. The eyes widen. The colour deepens. The mouth falls open like a fish's and stays open. It was so with Joe now.

'Red book?' he stammered.

'Red book.'

'Little red book?'

'Little red book.'

'Little red book of telephone numbers?'

'Little red book of telephone numbers.'

The sensation of having been struck with a wet towel left Joe. He became indignant, like a good man unjustly persecuted.

'Why the dickens does everybody make such a song and dance about my little red book of telephone numbers?' he demanded hotly. 'Every red-blooded man has his little red book of telephone numbers. Children start keeping them in the kindergarten. And Kay knows all about my little red book. I explained carefully and fully to her the last time we lunched together that no importance whatsoever was to be attached to that little red book. I told her that the girls in that little red book were mere vestiges of a past that is dead and gone. I've forgotten half their damned names. They are nothing to me, nothing.'

'Less than the dust beneath your chariot wheels?'

'Considerably less. I wouldn't ring one of them up to please a dying grandmother. They're ghosts, I tell you. Spectres. Wraiths.'

'Just wisps of ectoplasm?'

'Exactly. Just wisps of ectoplasm. Listen, Bill. There isn't a girl that exists for me in the world except Kay. She stands alone. Turn me loose on a street corner and have Helen of Troy, Cleopatra, Mrs Langtry, Hedy Lamarr and La Belle Dame Sans Merci parade past me in one-piece bathing suits, and I wouldn't even bother to whistle at them.'

Bill was touched by his simple eloquence.

'Well, that sounds pretty satisfactory. Summing it up, then, you are as pure as the driven snow?'

'If not purer.'

'Good. Then all you have to do, as I see it, is to change the radio comic approach. You can't run a business that way. Cut the Bob Hope stuff down to a minimum. There are two methods of winning a girl's heart,' said Bill. 'The first is to be the dominant male – the caveman, and take her heart by storm. As an illustration of what I mean, I once wrote for *Passion Magazine* where the hero was no end of a character. He was one of the huntin', ridin' and shootin' set of Old Westbury, Long Island, and he had dark, sullen fits of rage, under the influence of which he would grab his girl by the back hair and drag her about the room with clenched teeth. His teeth were clenched, of course, not hers. Hers just rattled. I throw this out as a suggestion.'

'I'm not going to drag Kay about rooms by her hair.'

'It would be a delicate attention. It might just turn the scale. The girl in my story loved it. "Oh, Gerald, Gerald," she said, "you do something to me."'

'No.'

'All right, then, cut business with hair. But you could seize her by the shoulders and shake her like a rat.'

'No, I couldn't.'

'Why not?'

'Because I couldn't.'

'You're a difficult fellow to help,' said Bill. 'You don't meet one half-way. You seem to have forgotten the old Superba-Llewellyn slogan, Service and Co-operation.'

She took the Mickey Finn from her pocket and joggled it thoughtfully in the palm of her hand.

'What's that?' asked Joe.

'An aspirin. I sleep badly. Well, if you won't be a caveman, we must try the second method and melt her heart instead of storming it. We must build you up for sympathy.'

'How do you mean?'

'It's quite simple ... Thirsty work, these conferences. How about a refresher?'

'That sounds like a good idea. Champagne?'

'I think so. Stick to the old and tried.'

Bill went to the tray, filled two glasses and adroitly dropped the present from her Third Avenue bartender friend into the one which she handed to Joe.

'Yes,' she said. 'We must build you up for sympathy.'

'But how?'

'It's quite simple.'

'You said that before.'

'And I say it again. You know the old poem, "Oh, woman, in our hours of ease ..."'

'"Uncertain, coy and hard to please ..." Yes, I used to recite it as a kid.'

'It must have sounded wonderful. Why do I miss these things? Well, you remember, then, that we have it straight from the horse's mouth that it requires only a little pain and anguish wringing the brow to turn a girl into a ministering angel. "When pain and anguish wring the brow, a ministering angel, thou." It's all in the book of words.'

'So what?'

'Well, take the case of Kay. I am convinced that if Kay, who is now down in the kitchen cutting wholesome sandwiches, were to come in here and find you lying prone and senseless on the floor, her heart would melt like a nut sundae in the Sahara desert. She would fling herself on your prostrate form and shower kisses on your upturned face. That's what Kay would do, if she came in here and found you lying prone and senseless on the floor.'

'But why would I be lying prone and senseless on the floor?'

Bill nodded. She saw what he meant.

'Yes, that wants thinking out. Well, suppose Phipps in a fit of drunken fury had knocked you cold with that bottle he is nursing as a mother nurses her child?'

'But he hasn't.'

'True. Then suppose I had slipped a Mickey Finn in that drink of yours.'

'But you didn't.'

'True, true. I'm just thinking aloud. Well, here's luck.'

'Luck,' said Joe.

They drained their glasses.

'Mickey Finn,' said Bill pensively, 'I wonder why those things are called that?'

'Wasn't there supposed to have been a bartender named Mickey Finn who invented them?'

'Mencken says not, and he probably knows. Mencken knows everything. Any idea how they work?'

'Yes, oddly enough, I have. It came up in a picture I was doing just before they fired me. Apparently you feel no ill effects at first. Then, if you shake your head – like this . . .'

Bill, quick on her feet, caught him as he started to fall. She lowered him gently to the floor, gave him a look in which commiseration and satisfaction were nicely blended, then crossed to the sofa and shook Phipps by the shoulder.

It is never easy to rouse an intoxicated butler who is in the process of sleeping off two Wilhelmina Shannon Specials and a bottle of *crème de menthe*, and for some time it seemed as though

her efforts were to be unrewarded. But presently signs of anima-
tion began to appear in the rigid limbs. Phipps grunted. He
stirred, he moved, he seemed to feel the rush of life along his
keel. Another grunt, and he sat up, blinking.

'Hullo?' he said, speaking in a husky whisper, like a spirit at a
séance. 'What goes on?'

'I am sorry to disturb your slumbers, Mr Phipps,' said Bill apologetically, 'but I can't seem to bring him to.'

'Eh?'

Bill indicated the remains on the floor.

'Perhaps you could lend a hand?' she said. 'Two heads are better than one.'

Phipps rose unsteadily from the sofa. It appeared to his dis-ordered senses that there was a body on the carpet, as had so often happened in the whodunits which were his favourite read-ing. In those works it was almost impossible to come into a room without finding bodies on the carpet. The best you could say of this one was that there was not a dagger of Oriental design stick-ing in its back. He closed his eyes, hoping that this might cause the cadaver to disappear. But when he opened them, it was still there.

'What's the matter with him?' he quavered. 'What's he lying there for?'

Bill raised her eyebrows.

'Surely you recall that, doubtless with the best motives, you socked him on the occiput with your bottle?'

'My – Gawd! Did I?'

'Don't tell me you've forgotten?'

'I can't remember a thing,' said the butler pallidly. 'What happened?'

'Well, it started with you getting into an argument about the Claims to Apostolic Succession of the Church of Abyssinia.'

'About *what*?'

'Don't you remember the Church of Abyssinia?'

'I never heard of the Church of Abyssinia.'

'Well, it's a sort of church they have out Abyssinia way and you and Joe Davenport got arguing about its claims to Apostolic Succession. He took one view, you took another. You said this, he said that. Hot words ensued. Angry passions rose. You gradually bumped him with the bottle. A crash, a cry, and smiling the boy fell dead.'

'He's not *dead*?'

'I was only making a good story of it.'

'Well, I wish you wouldn't,' said Phipps, passing a hand across his ashen forehead. He collapsed into a chair and sat puffing unhappily. He was still doing so when the door opened and Smedley came in, followed by Kay, who was carrying a large plate of sandwiches, at which Bill looked with an approving eye. She was feeling just about ready for a little snack.

'Adela must be asleep,' said Smedley. 'I stood outside her door for quite a time, listening, but I couldn't hear anything. Hello,' he went on, Joe having caught his eye. 'What's this?'

'Stretcher case,' said Bill briefly. 'Phipps hit him with a bottle. We were just chatting about it when you came in.'

Kay's eyes widened. The blood slowly left her face. She stood for an instant, staring, and the plate of sandwiches trembled in her hand. Bill, always doing the right thing, took it gently from her. Kay seemed to come to life. With a cry she flung herself beside Joe's prostrate form.

'Oh, Joe, Joe!' she wailed.

Bill helped herself to a sandwich with a quick, gratified smile. It is always pleasant for a kind-hearted woman who wants to bring the young folks together in springtime to see that she has succeeded in doing so. She finished the sandwich and took another. Sardine, she was glad to note. She liked sardine sandwiches.

'Hit him with a bottle?' said Smedley.

'In a moment of heat,' Bill explained. 'The Phippses get very heated at moments.'

'Good God!'

'Yes, a disagreeable thing to have happened. Spoiled the party, as you might say. But there is a bright side. It has had the effect of sobering him.'

'It has? Then listen ...'

'I believe he's dead,' said Kay, raising a white face.

'Oh, I shouldn't think so,' said Smedley. He dismissed this side issue and returned to the important subject. 'He's sober, is he?'

'Quite. He could say truly rural.'

'Then now's the time for him to get to work. No more fooling about. Phipps!'

'Sir?' said that reveller, now once more his old respectful butlerine self.

'Get busy.'

'Yes, sir.'

'No more nonsense.'

'No, sir.'

'His master's voice,' said Bill, starting on her third sandwich.

Kay, she saw with approval, was now showering burning kisses on Joe's upturned face. This, it will be remembered, was the business she had arranged for her, and it was nice to see it working out so smoothly. She felt like a director whose cast is on its toes and giving of its best.

'Oh, Joe! Joe, darling!' cried Kay. She looked up. 'He's alive.'

'Really?'

'He just moved.'

'Fine,' said Bill. 'This is excellent news. No electric chair for you this time, Phipps.'

'I am relieved, madam.'

'Later on, perhaps.'

'Yes, madam.'

Kay was glaring balefully. Hitherto, she had always liked Phipps, but now it seemed to her that she had never met a beastlier butler.

'You might have killed him,' she said. She spoke bitterly and with clenched teeth, like Bill's huntin', ridin' and shootin' friend from Old Westbury, and would have hissed the words if there had been an 's' in them.

Phipps, still respectful, disputed this point.

'I would not go so far as to say that, miss. Just a simple slosh on the head, such as so often occurs during a religious argument. But if I might be permitted to say so, I would like to express regret and contrition for having taken such a liberty. From the bottom of me heart, miss . . .'

Smedley broke in with his usual impatience. He was in no mood for oratory.

'Now don't stand there making speeches. This isn't the Fourth of July.'

'No, sir.'

'Action, man, action.'

'Yes, sir.'

'Follow me.'

'Yes, sir. Very good, sir.'

The door closed behind them. Bill smiled maternally at Kay and joined her at the sick-bed. She looked down at the invalid, who was now showing definite signs of coming out of his coma.

'He'll be functioning again in a minute,' she said encouragingly. 'Bet you ten cents I know what he'll say when he opens his eyes. "Where am I?"'

Joe opened his eyes.

'Where am I?' he asked.

'Gimme those ten cents,' said Bill.

Joe sat up.

'Oh, gosh!' he said.

'Oh, Joe!' said Kay.

'My head!' said Joe.

'Painful, no doubt,' said Bill. 'What you need is air. We'll get you into the garden. Lend me a hand, Kay.'

'I'll bathe your head, darling,' said Kay tenderly.

Joe blinked.

'Did you say "darling"?'

'Of course I did.'

Joe blinked again.

'And just now ... Was it just a lovely dream, or did you kiss me?'

'Of course she kissed you,' said Bill. 'Why wouldn't she kiss you? Weren't you listening when I told you she loves you? Can you navigate?'

'I think so.'

'Then we'll take you out and bathe your head in Adela's jewelled swimming pool.'

Joe blinked for the third time. Even so trivial a muscular effort as blinking affected his head as if some earnest hand were driving red-hot spikes into it, but the agony, though acute, was forgotten in the thrill of ecstasy which shot through him. It seemed to him once again that soft music was playing in the Garden Room. Familiar objects had taken on a new beauty. Even Bill's rugged face, which good judges had compared to that of a German Boxer, now showed itself as something entitling her to get her telephone number into the most discriminating man's little red book.

As for Kay, the thought struck him that if you slapped a pair of wings on her, she could step straight into any gathering of Cherubim and Seraphim and no questions asked. He gazed at her in a stunned way.

'You love me?'

'Certainly she loves you,' said Bill. 'How many times have I to keep telling you? She worships you. She adores you. She would die for one little rose from your hair. But you'll be able to discuss all that while she's ducking your head in the swimming pool. Come along, and take it easy. I'll bet you're feeling like someone who has annoyed Errol Flynn.'

Supporting the injured man between them, they passed through the french windows. And scarcely had they disappeared when the door opened and Adela came in, followed by a limp and drowsy Lord Topham. Adela was alert and bristling, her escort practically walking in his sleep. He tottered to a chair, sank into it and closed his eyes.

CHAPTER 15

The trouble about going up to a sister-in-law's room and listening at her door to make sure she is asleep is that, if your breathing is at all inclined to be stertorous, you are apt to wake her. Although he was not aware of it, Smedley on his recent visit to the exterior of Adela's sleeping apartment had breathed very stertorously. What with the strain of being accessory before the fact to a safeblowing and the emotional disturbance occasioned by hearing Phipps address him as old drunken Smedley, he had puffed and panted like a racehorse at the conclusion of a stiff Grand National.

He had also caused boards to creak and once, over-balancing, had brought his hand sharply against the panel of the door. Indeed, practically the only thing he had not done was to make a noise like an alarm clock, and he had been operating less than a minute and a half when Adela stirred on her pillow, sat up and finally, hearing that bang on the door, got up. With the air of an Amazon donning her armour before going into battle, she put on a dressing-gown and stood listening.

The sounds outside had ceased. A cautious peep a moment later showed that nobody was there. But somebody had been there, and she proposed to look into the matter thoroughly. There was nothing of the poltroon about Adela Shannon Cork. Any one of a dozen silent picture directors could have told you that, and so could each of her three late husbands. As has previously been indicated, she was a woman who stood no nonsense, and under the head of nonsense she classed the presence of unlawful intruders in her house between the hours of one and two in the morning.

But even the most intrepid of women likes on such an occasion as this to have an ally, so after the briefest of delays she proceeded to Lord Topham's room, and with much more difficulty than Smedley had experienced in waking her, roused him to at least a temporary activity.

He appeared now to have turned in again for the night, and she addressed him sharply.

'Lord Topham!'

Gentle breathing was her guest's only reply. Lord Topham was a man who, though resembling Napoleon Bonaparte in no other way, shared with him the ability to drop off the moment his head touched the pillow – or, as in the present case, the back of a chair.

She raised her voice.

'Lord Topham!'

The mists of sleep were not proof against that urgent cry. The visitor from across the seas opened his eyes. Napoleon in similar circumstances would probably have opened his. Adela's voice lacked the booming thunderousness of Bill's, but it was very penetrating when annoyance caused her to raise it.

'Eh?'

'Wake up.'

'Was I asleep?'

'Yes, you were.'

Lord Topham considered the point, remembered that a moment ago he had been dancing the rhumba in Piccadilly Circus, and nodded.

'That's right. I was. I was dreaming of Toots.'

'Of *what?*'

'Girl I know in London. I dreamed that we were treading the measure in Piccadilly Circus. Of all places. Well, I mean to say,' said Lord Topham, smiling a little at the quaint idea, 'would one? In Piccadilly Circus, I mean to say, what?'

Adela was not a psychiatrist, ever ready to listen to people's dreams and interpret them. She made no comment other than an impatient sniff. Then she uttered a sharp exclamation. Her eye, roving about the room, had fallen on the tray of bottles.

'Look!'

Lord Topham sighed sentimentally.

'I'll tell you about Toots. I love her like billy-o, and we had a row just before I sailed for America. She's a sweet girl—'

'Look at those bottles!'

'– but touchy.'

'Who put those bottles there?'

'Very touchy. A queen of her sex, but touchy. Absolutely.'

'Who – put – those – bottles – there? I was right. There are burglars in the house.'

Lord Topham heaved another sigh. This seemed to him about as good a time as any to unbare his soul concerning the tragedy which had been darkening it.

'Takes offence rather readily, if you know what I mean, though an angel in every possible respect. You'll scarcely believe this, but just because I told her her new hat made her look like Boris Karloff, she hauled off and biffed me on the side of the head, observing as she did so that she never wanted to see or speak to me again in this world or the next. Well, a fellow has his pride, what? I admit I drew myself up to my full height—'

'Be quiet. Listen.'

Adela's gaze had shifted to the ceiling. A muffled sound had proceeded from the projection room above. This was because Smedley, becoming conscious of an imperious desire for a restorative and knowing that all the materials were downstairs, had started for the door and tripped over a footstool.

'There is someone in the projection room. Lord Topham! . . . LORD TOPHAM!'

Lord Topham woke, like Abou ben Adhem, from a deep dream of peace. There crossed his mind the passing thought that he was having a rather disturbed night.

'Hullo?'

'Go up.'

'Where?'

'Upstairs.'

'Why?'

'There are burglars in the projection room.'

'Then I'm dashed if I'm going there,' said Lord Topham. 'I was about to tell you, when I dozed off, that I wrote Toots a well-expressed air mail letter the day before yesterday, saying that the fault was mine and pleading for a reconciliation. I'd look a silly ass going and getting bumped off by a bunch of bally burglars before I had time to get an answer. What? Well, I mean to say! I'm expecting a cable any moment.'

Many people would have approved of his attitude. A prudent and sensible young man, they would have said, with his head screwed on the right way. But Adela could not see eye to eye with them. She uttered an indignant snort and prowled restlessly about the room like a caged lioness. It was not long before she discovered the open french window.

'Lord Topham!'

'Now what?'

'The window is open.'

'The window?'

'The window.'

'Open?'

'Yes.'

Lord Topham, though drowsy, could grasp a simple point like this. With a brief 'The window? Oh, ah, the window. You mean the window?' he looked in the direction indicated.

'Yes,' he said. 'Absolutely. Quite. I see exactly what you mean. Open as per esteemed memo. Did you say that there were burglars in the house?'

'Yes.'

'Then mark my words, that's how they got in,' said Lord Topham, and went to sleep.

And there's someone coming along the corridor!' cried Adela, stiffening from head to foot. 'Lord Topham ... LORD TOPHAM!!'

'I say, must you? What's the matter now?'

'I can hear someone coming along the corridor.'

'No, really? Well, well.'

Adela snatched a bottle from the table and pressed it into her companion's hand. He peered at it as if, though this was far from being the case, he were seeing a bottle for the first time.

'What's this?'

'You will need a weapon.'

'Who, me?'

'Yes.'

'A weapon?'

'Yes.'

'Why?'

'The moment he appears, strike him with it.'

'Who?'

'The man in the corridor.'

'But I don't want to go striking men in corridors.'

The door opened, revealing a portly form, at the sight of which Adela's pent-up emotions released themselves in an exasperated scream.

'Smedley!' she cried.

'Oof!' cried Smedley.

'Do I strike him?' inquired Lord Topham.

'What on earth,' said Adela, 'are you doing wandering about the house at this time of night, Smedley?'

Smedley stood in the doorway, gulping painfully and endeavouring with little success to adjust himself to the severest of all the shocks which had tried his morale in the course of this night of terror. It is not pleasant for a nervous man who comes into a room expecting a Bourbon highball to find there a sister-in-law who even under the most favourable conditions has always made him feel like a toad beneath the harrow.

He continued to gulp. Strange wordless sounds proceeded from his pallid lips. His resemblance to the sheeted dead who squeaked and gibbered in the Roman streets a little 'ere the mightiest Julius fell was extraordinarily close, though to Lord Topham, who was unfamiliar with the play in which this powerful image occurs, he suggested more a cat about to have a fit. In his boyhood Lord Topham had owned a large tortoiseshell which had distressed himself and family by behaving just as Smedley was behaving now.

To ease the strain, he repeated his question.

'Do I strike him?'

'No.'

'Not strike him?'

'No.'

'Right ho,' said Lord Topham agreeably. 'I merely asked.'

Adela glared.

'Well, Smedley?'

Smedley at last found speech.

'I – I couldn't sleep. What – what brings you here? Adela?'

'I heard noises outside my room. Footsteps, and someone breathing. I woke Lord Topham and we came down and saw those bottles.'

Smedley, still almost too shocked for utterance, contrived with an effort to keep the conversation going.

'Bottles?'

'Bottles.'

'Oh, yes ... Bottles. I ... I think Phipps must have put them there,' said Smedley, casting an agonized glance at the ceiling.

Adela uttered an impatient 'Tchah!' She had never had a high opinion of her brother-in-law's intelligence, but tonight he seemed to have sunk to new depths of idiocy.

'What in the name of goodness would Phipps be doing, strewing five hundred and fifty-seven bottles about the room?'

'Butlers do put bottles all over the place,' urged Smedley.

Lord Topham endorsed this dictum. His had been a life into which butlers had entered rather largely, and he knew their habits.

'Absolutely. Quite. He's right. They do, I mean, what? They're noted for it. Bottles, bottles everywhere, in case you want a drink.'

Adela snorted. It was a hard thing to say of anyone, but in her opinion Lord Topham's mentality was about equal to Smedley's.

'And I suppose it's Phipps making those noises in the projection room?' she said witheringly.

Smedley uttered a cry of agony. He was so used to tripping over footstools or his feet or anything that was handy that it had not occurred to him that there had been noises in the projection room. If Adela had heard such noises, it seemed to him that it would be only a matter of moments before she was up and tracing them to their source. And then what?

He stood there, squeaking and gibbering, completely at a loss as to how to deal with the appalling situation. Then relief flooded his soul. Bill was coming in through the french window, looking so solid, so dependable that, if only faintly, hope stirred in its winding cloths. It might be that matters had reached such a pass as to be beyond the power of human control, but if anyone could take arms against this sea of troubles and by opposing end them, it was good old Bill.

Adela beheld her sister with less pleasure.

'Wilhelmina!'

'Oh, hello, Adela. Hello, Smedley. Pip-pip, Lord Topham.'

'Toodle-oo, Miss Shannon. Do I strike her?' he asked, for it seemed silly to him to have been issued equipment – bottle, one, people striking for use of – and not to employ it in action.

'Oh, be quiet,' snapped Adela. 'What are you doing here, Wilhelmina?'

'Just strolling. I couldn't sleep. What are you?'

'I heard noises.'

'Imagination.'

'It was not imagination. There is someone in the projection room.'

A tenseness came upon Bill. Not so good, this, she was feeling, not so good. She divined, correctly, that Smedley must have been falling over himself and raising enough uproar to wake the whole populace within miles. Phipps, that silent artist, she acquitted of blame.

'Someone in the projection room?'

'I heard the floor creaking.'

'Mice.'

'Mice be damned. It's a burglar.'

'Have you been up there?'

'Of course I haven't. I don't want the top of my head blown off.'

'Precisely how I feel,' said Lord Topham. 'I was explaining to our dear good hostess here that just before I left England I had a row with my girl Toots, and I've written her a well-expressed air mail letter pleading for a reconciliation and am expecting a reply at any moment, so naturally I am reluctant to get the old lemon blown into hash by nocturnal marauders before that reply arrives – a reply, I may say, which I am hoping will be favourable. True, I left the dear sweet creature foaming rather freely at the mouth and tearing my photographs up and stamping on them, but what I always say is that Time, the great healer—'

'Oh, be quiet!'

'Poor Lord Topham,' said Bill. 'You get about as much chance to talk in this house as a parrot living with Tallulah Bankhead. You had a row with your girl, did you?'

'A frightful row. Battle of the century. It was about her new hat, which I described – injudiciously, I see now, as making her look like—'

'Lord Topham!'

'Hullo?'

Adela spoke with a strained calm.

'I do not wish to hear about your friend Toots.'

'But is she my friend? That's the moot point.'

'To hell and damnation with your blasted Toots!' cried Adela, reverting, as she so often did in moments of emotion, to the breezy *argot* of the old silent film days, when a girl had to be able to express herself if she wanted to get anywhere. Her calm had exploded into fragments. She could not have regarded the young peer with more stormy distaste if she had caught him trying to steal a scene from her. 'Will you kindly stop talking about this miserable creature, who has probably got platinum hair and a lisp and is the scum of the underworld. All I am interested in at the moment is that burglar in the projection room.'

Bill shook her head.

'There isn't a burglar in the projection room.'

'I tell you there is.'

'Shall I go and investigate?'

'What good would you be? No, we'll wait for the police.'

Smedley collapsed on the sofa. This was the end.

'Per-per-police?'

'I telephoned them from my bedroom. Why they are not here is more than I can imagine. I suppose they're walking. It would be just like those half-witted imbeciles they call policemen in Beverly Hills to ... Ah!' said Adela. 'And about time.'

A sergeant and a patrolman were coming through the french window.

CHAPTER 16

The sergeant was a tough, formidable sergeant, who looked as if he had been hewn from the living rock. The patrolman was a tough, formidable patrolman, who gave the same impression. They came in with the measured tread of men conscious of their ability to uphold the Law and make the hardiest criminal say Uncle.

'Good evening, ma'am,' said the sergeant.

Adela was still in difficult mood. Women of her wealth grow to expect their orders to be filled with speed and promptness.

'Good evening,' she said. 'You've taken your time coming. What were you doing? Playing Canasta?'

The sergeant seemed wounded.

'Came as quick as we could, ma'am. You're reporting a burglary?'

Adela gave him a full whammy.

'Don't they tell you *anything* at police headquarters? Yes, as I went to the trouble of explaining carefully over the telephone, there are burglars in the house. They are up in the projection room.'

'Where's that?'

'The room immediately above this one. Smedley, show the officers up to the projection room.'

Smedley quivered like a Roman Emperor hearing the leader of the band of assassins which has just filed into his private apartments say 'Well, here we are, Galba' – or Vitellius or Caligula or whatever the name might be. He cast an imploring glance at Bill, as if pleading with her not to fail him in this dark hour.

Bill, as always, did her best.

'There aren't any burglars in the projection room. Absurd.'

'Absurd, my foot. I heard strange noises.'

Bill caught the sergeant's eye. Her own twinkled.

'She heard strange noises, sergeant. Ha, ha. We women! Poor, timid, fluttering creatures.'

'Listen! Any time *I* flutter . . .'

'Just bundles of nerves, aren't we, sergeant?'

'Yes, ma'am. My wife's like that.'

'My wife's like that,' said the patrolman.

'All women are like that,' said Bill. 'It's something to do with the bone structure of our heads.'

The sergeant said Maybe you're right, ma'am. The patrolman said Yes, she had a point there. His wife, said the patrolman, was a great believer in omens and portents and would you ever catch that woman walking under a ladder, no, ma'am: and the sergeant said his wife always said 'Rabbits, rabbits, rabbits' on the first day of the month, because she held the view that if you said 'Rabbits, rabbits, rabbits' on the first day of the month, you got a present within the next two weeks. Silly, said the sergeant, but there it was.

'Listen,' said Adela, who was showing signs of becoming overwrought.

'Just a moment, Adela,' said Bill. 'Sit down,' she said to the arms of the Law, 'and tell us all about your wives.'

It was a tempting offer, and for a moment the sergeant seemed to waver. But a splendid spirit animates the police force of Beverly Hills, and he was strong again.

'Not just now, ma'am,' he said. 'I guess we'd best take a look at this projection room the lady wants us to take a look at.'

'Waste of time,' said Bill judicially.

'Yes,' agreed Smedley, speaking with a feverish earnestness. 'And you wouldn't like the projection room. Honestly.'

'Besides, there's no hurry,' said Bill. 'Good heavens, the night's yet young. Take a couple of chairs and have a drink.'

A passer-by at this point might have supposed that an ammunition dump had exploded in the near neighbourhood. But it was only Adela.

'Sweet suffering soup-spoons!' cried Adela, raising her hands to heaven in a passionate gesture. 'Take a couple of chairs! Have a drink! What *is* this? A college reunion?'

The sergeant shook his head. The bottles on the tray had not escaped his notice, for the police are trained to observe, and his eye had gleamed at the suggestion that he should investigate their contents. It was a pity, he felt, that this admirable woman who looked like a German Boxer was not in charge of the proceedings. Bill, in his opinion, had nice ideas, and it would have been a pleasure to fall in with them. But apparently it was this other dame, whose face seemed oddly familiar for some reason, who was directing operations, and her views were less in keeping with the trend of modern thought.

'No, thank you, ma'am,' he said virtuously. 'Not while we're on duty. Come on, Bill.'

'Is your name Bill?' said Bill.

The patrolman said it was, and Bill said Well, well, well.

'So is mine,' said Bill. 'What an amazing coincidence. Let's curl up on the sofa and have a long talk about it.'

'Later on, ma'am,' said the sergeant. He glanced up at the ceiling, and there came into his face that keen look which policemen wear when constabulary duty is to be done. 'Seems to me I do hear something up there,' he said. 'A kind of creaking noise.'

'All very old houses creak at night,' said Bill. 'This one, I believe, dates back to the early Cecil B. de Mille period.'

'Ask me,' said the patrolman, 'it's more like a sort of scratching sound.'

Bill cocked an ear.

'Ah, yes,' she said. 'I know what that is. That is my sister's poodle. He has a sensitive skin, and he is like the young lady of Natchez, who said: "Where Ah itches, Ah scratches." Are you fond of dogs, sergeant?'

'Yes, ma'am. I've a dog at home—'

'What sort?'

'A Scotty, ma'am.'

'No nicer breed. Very intelligent animals, Scotties.'

'Intelligent? You said it. Say, listen,' said the sergeant.

'Say, listen,' said the patrolman, who wanted to speak of his Boston terrier, Buster.

'Say, listen,' said Adela, who had been fermenting rather freely during these exchanges. 'Listen, you Keystone Kops, are you or are you not going up to that projection room?'

'Sure, lady, sure,' said the sergeant. 'Come on, Bill.'

They started for the door, and Smedley uttered the soft little moan of despair of the man who feels that the doom has come upon him. Tripping over his feet, he fell against the sergeant, who fell against Adela, who asked him what he imagined he was playing at. Football? inquired Adela. Or Postman's Knock?

'Pardon, lady,' said the sergeant courteously. 'The gentleman bumped me.' He paused, staring. 'Say, aren't you Adela Shannon?'

'I am.'

'Well, I'll be a son-of-a,' said the sergeant. 'I seen you in the old silents. You remember Adela Shannon, Bill?'

'Sure,' said the patrolman. 'She used to be the Empress of Stormy Emotion.'

'She still is,' said Bill. 'So you're interested in pictures, are you, sergeant?'

'Yes, ma'am. Are you connected with pix?'

'No longer. I had a job with Superba-Llewellyn, but they fired me.'

'Too bad. Still, that's how it goes.'

'That's how it goes.'

The patrolman laughed a bitter laugh.

'Yes, that's how it goes – in Hollywood,' he said. 'Ha!'

Bill looked at him, interested. She turned to the sergeant.

'He doesn't seem to like Hollywood.'

'No, ma'am.'

Adela clenched her teeth. Her fists were already clenched. She spoke with the strained sweetness of a woman who is holding herself in with all the resolution at her disposal, knowing that if she relaxes for an instant, she will spring into the air, howling like a Banshee. No less than Smedley, who was now a mere jelly, she was finding the proceedings something of a strain. The zealous officers were affecting her like a Viennese director she remembered from the old days, a man at whose head she had once been compelled in the interests of her art to throw one of the swords used by the Roman soldiers in *Hail, Caesar*.

'Might I have your attention for a moment, Mr Louis B. Mayer, and you, Mr Zanuck,' she said. 'Do you intend during the next hour or so to get some action, or is this conference going on for ever? Did you come here to arrest burglars or just to chat about motion pictures? I merely wish to know how matters stand?' said Adela, all charm and consideration.

Bill rebuked her gently.

'You're so impatient, Adela. We have the night before us. Why doesn't your friend like Hollywood?'

The sergeant's brow darkened.

'He tried for a job at Medulla-Oblongata-Glutz last week, and they turned him down on account he wanted to do whimsical comedy and they said he wasn't right for whimsical comedy.'

'You're kidding me.'

'No, ma'am, that's what they said.'

'Astounding. He looks all right for whimsical comedy to *me*.'

'Sure I'm all right for whimsical comedy,' said the patrolman. 'But it's all a closed ring. That's what it is, just a closed ring. If you're new talent, you haven't a chance.'

'It's tough,' said Bill.

'You're right, it's tough,' said the sergeant. 'Say, listen. When I tried to muscle in at Colossal-Superhuman, they had the nerve to say I lacked dramatic intensity.'

'It's incredible.'

A sigh like the wind blowing through the cracks in a broken heart escaped Adela. Her spirit was broken.

'God give me strength!' she moaned. 'I telephone for policemen, and they send me a couple of ham actors. I shall go to bed. Lord Topham ... LORD TOPHAM!'

Lord Topham sat up, blinking.

'Hullo? Is that Toots?'

Adela was silent for a moment. She seemed to be swallowing something.

'No,' she said at length, speaking with some difficulty. 'It is not Toots. Lord Topham, you have been about as much use up to now as a pain in the neck. Would it be too much to ask you to accompany me to my bedroom?'

'Accompany you to your—?'

'With burglars in every nook and cranny of the house, I don't propose to go up two flights of stairs alone.'

Lord Topham seemed relieved.

'Oh, yes, yes, yes, yes, yes,' he said. 'I thought for a moment … Ha, ha, silly of me. Absolutely. Yes, yes, yes, yes, of course. I see what you mean.'

'Bring that bottle.'

'Eh? Oh, the jolly old bottle? Quite, quite.'

'And any time you get through talking about your dramatic intensity,' said Adela, addressing the sergeant, 'you will find the burglars in the projection room. I'll shout through the door and tell them to be sure to wait. Come, Lord Topham.'

'Ladies first,' said Lord Topham gallantly.

'Ladies first, my left eyeball,' said Adela. 'Why, they may be lurking in the corridor.'

Lord Topham went out, followed by Adela. The sergeant, who appeared to have been stung by her parting words, became active.

'Come on, let's go.'

'Oh, not yet,' begged Smedley.

'Yes, sir. We have our duty to do.'

'But I want to hear all about this gentleman's whimsical comedy,' said Bill. 'Do sit down and have a drink.'

'Thank you, no, ma'am.'

'Say when.'

'When,' said the sergeant.

'You?'

'Not for me, ma'am.'

'Say when.'

'When,' said the patrolman.

'That's better,' said Bill. 'Now we're set. Now we're cosy. Why did Medulla-Oblongata-Glutz think you were not right for whimsical comedy?'

'Search me,' said the patrolman, moodily. 'What's Clark Gable got that I haven't got?'

'A moustache, ten million dollars and Lady Sylvia Ashley.'

The sergeant saw that there had been a misunderstanding.

'He is alluding to talent, ma'am.'

'Oh, talent?'

'Yes, talent,' said the patrolman. 'I got talent. I know it. I feel it *here*,' said the patrolman, slapping his chest.

Bill cocked an eye at the sergeant.

'You have talent, too?'

'Sure I got talent,' said the sergeant. 'And who says I lack dramatic intensity? Listen. "Drop that gun, you rat. You know me. Tough Tom Hennessy, the cop that always gets his man. Ah, would you? Bang, bang." That's where I shoot and plug him,' explained the sergeant. 'It's a little thing I threw together with a view to showing myself in a dramatic role. There's more of it, but that'll give you the idea.'

'It's wonderful,' said Bill. 'A poignant and uplifting cameo of life as it is lived today, purifying the emotions with pity and terror.'

The sergeant simpered modestly, one massive foot drawing circles on the carpet.

'Thanks, ma'am.'

'Not at all.'

'Care to look in at the station house some day, I'll show you my stills.'

'I can hardly wait.'

'Yes, ma'am, that's the sort of thing I can do. But they turn me down.'

'That's Hollywood.'

'That's Hollywood.'

'You're right, that's Hollywood,' said the patrolman. 'Lookit, ma'am. Watch. What's this?'

He smiled.

'Joy?' said Bill.

'Joy is right. And this?'

He tightened his lips.

'Grief!'

'Grief is right. And this?'

He raised his eyebrows.

'Horror?'

'You betcher, horror. And I can do hate, too. But it's whimsical comedy I'm best at. Like where the fellow meets the girl and starts kidding her. But could I drive that into their thick skulls at M-O-G? No, ma'am. They turned me down.'

'That's Hollywood,' said Bill.

'That's Hollywood,' said the sergeant.

'You're right, that's Hollywood,' said the patrolman.

'Bright city of sorrows,' said Bill. 'Ah, Phipps.'

The butler had come shimmering through the door. If he felt any surprise or alarm at observing policemen on the premises, he gave no sign of it. He was his usual dignified self.

'I came to see if there was anything more you required, madam.'

'Not a thing, thank you,' said Bill.

'Say, who's this?' said the sergeant.

'My sister's butler. Sergeant—?'

'Ward, ma'am. And Patrolman Morehouse.'

'Thank you. Mr Phipps. Sergeant Ward and Patrolman Morehouse.'

'How do you do?' said Phipps.

'Pleased to meet you,' said the sergeant.

'Hi!' said the patrolman, also indicating pleasure.

Bill showed a womanly concern for the butler's well-being.

'You're up late, Phipps. Couldn't you sleep, either?'

'No, madam. I experienced an annoying wakefulness. Most unusual with me, madam.'

'You should have tried counting sheep.'

'I did, madam, but without avail. So finally, I took the liberty of proceeding to the projection room and running off *Forever Amber.*'

The sergeant uttered an exclamation.

'What's that? Was it you in that projection room?'

'Yes, sir.'

It was plain that the sergeant now saw it all. His trained mind had leaped to the significance of the butler's story.

'Then there you are. There you have the whole mystery explained and the case cleaned up. The lady thought it was burglars.'

'Mrs Cork,' explained Bill. 'She has just left us. She heard noises and became alarmed.'

'I am sorry, madam. I endeavoured to be as silent as possible.'

'I'm sure you did.'

The sergeant wiped his lips, and rose.

'Well, we'll be getting along. Good night, ma'am.'

'Good night. Take care of that dramatic intensity.'

'I will, ma'am.'

'And good luck to your artistic efforts.'

'Thank you, ma'am. But one kind of loses heart. The more you submit yourself to these casting offices, the more they give you the old runaround.'

'That's Hollywood.'

'That's Hollywood.'

'You're right, that's Hollywood,' said the patrolman. 'That tinsel town where tragedy lies hid behind a thousand false smiles, and—'

'Ah, come on,' said the sergeant.

Bill closed the french window behind them, and Smedley breathed the first carefree breath he had breathed since the dark doings of the night had begun.

'Bill,' he said, 'you're a marvel.'

'Thank you, Smedley. As Phipps would say, I desire to give satisfaction.'

'A marvel,' repeated Smedley. He turned to Phipps. 'Those cops were going up to the projection room, but she kept them talking and headed them off.'

'Indeed sir? The experience must have occasioned you a great deal of anxiety, madam.'

'Yes, it was a close thing,' said Bill. 'Lucky they were interested in pictures.'

Joe and Kay came in through the french window.

'Joe's feeling better,' said Kay.

'Good. And you look radiant.'

'Can you wonder?' said Joe. 'She's going to marry *me*.'

'Ah, you fixed it up all right. I thought you would. Kay, an aunt's blessing.'

'Thank you, Bill.'

'In my opinion, nice work. You probably feel the same, Smedley?'

Smedley executed a brief dance step. It might have signified joy, but more probably irritation. Smedley lacked Patrolman Morehouse's skill in registering.

'Yes, yes, yes,' he said, 'but I haven't time to bother about that now. You got it, Phipps?'

'Sir?'

'The diary.'

'Oh, yes, sir. Without any difficulty.'

'Good work, Phipps,' said Joe.

'Thank you, sir.'

'Splendid, Phipps,' said Kay.

'Thank you, miss.'

'Gimme,' said Smedley.

A look of respectful regret came into the butler's face.

'I am sorry, sir, but what you suggest is not feasible, sir.'

Smedley stared.

'What do you mean? You said you had got it.'

'Yes, sir. And I propose to keep it.'

'What?'

'Yes, sir. Would there be anything further, sir? Thank you, sir. Good night.'

He shimmered out, leaving a stunned silence behind him.

'My God!' said Bill, the first to break it. 'Hijacked *again*!' She paused, wrestling with her feelings. 'Go on, Smedley,' she said at length. '*You* say it. I'm a lady.'

There are, as everybody knows, many ways of measuring time, and from the earliest ages learned men have argued earnestly in favour of their different systems, with not a little bad blood, one is sorry to say, arising between the representatives of the various schools of thought.

Hipparchus of Rhodes, for instance, who had his own ideas on the way time should be measured, once referred to Marinus of Tyre, who held different opinions, as 'Marinus the flat tyre', which, though extraordinarily witty, was pretty bitter: and when Purbach and Regiomontanus were told the views of Achmed Ibn Abdallah of Baghdad, they laughed themselves cross-eyed. Purbach, who was a hard nut, said that Achmed Ibn Abdallah knew about as much about measuring time as his grandmother's cat, a notoriously backward animal, and when kind-hearted Regiomontanus in his tolerant way urged that Ahmed Ibn was just a young fellow trying to get along and one ought not to judge him too harshly, Purbach said 'Oh, yeah?' and Regiomontanus said 'Yeah', and Purbach said Was that so, and Regiomontanus said Yes, that was so, and Purbach said Regiomontanus made him sick. It was their first quarrel.

Tycho Brahe, the eminent Dane, measured time by means of altitudes, quadrants, azimuths, cross-staves, armillary spheres and parallactic rules, and the general opinion in Denmark was that he had got the thing down cold. And then in 1863 along came Dollen with his *Die Zeitbestimmung Vermittelst Des Tragbaren Durchgangsinstruments Im Verticale Des Polarsterns* – a best seller in its day, subsequently made into a musical by Rodgers and Hammerstein, who called it *North Atlantic*, a much better marquee title – and proved that Tycho, by mistaking an azimuth for an armillary sphere one night after the annual dinner of the alumni of Copenhagen University, had got his calculations all wrong, throwing the whole thing back into the melting pot.

The truth is that time cannot be measured. To Smedley, slumped in his chair on the terrace on the following morning, it seemed to be standing still. Melancholy had marked him for her own, and each leaden moment that dragged itself by took on the semblance of an hour. To Phipps, on the other hand, chanting a gay air in his pantry, the golden minutes seemed to race. Tra-la, sang Phipps, and Tiddly-om-pom-pom. In all Beverly Hills there was, as of even date, no sunnier butler. Lord Topham had described the previous day as the maddest and merriest of all the glad new year, but it seemed to Phipps that the current one relegated it to second place. God was in His heaven and all was right with the world, he felt. A contract with Medulla-Oblongata-Glutz in one pocket and a fifty thousand dollar diary in the other – what more could a man want?

Well, the way his head was feeling after last night, perhaps a bromo-seltzer. He rose and mixed himself one. And as he drained it, singing between the sips like somebody in a drinking chorus in an opera, his eye fell on the clock. Nearly noon? Time for old Smedley's yoghurt.

Smedley had closed his eyes when the butler arrived on the

terrace, and was not aware of his presence till he spoke behind him.

'Good morning, sir,' said Phipps, and Smedley skipped as nearly like the high hills as is within the scope of a seated man.

'Oof!' he said. 'You startled me.'

'That will cure your hiccups, sir.'

'I don't have hiccups.'

'I am sorry, sir. I was not aware of that.'

Smedley, who had been in one of his daydreams, now realized for the first time that the voice which had broken in on his reverie was that of Southern California's most prominent viper. A viper to end all vipers.

'Well, viper,' he said, injecting a wealth of hate and abhorrence into the salutation and with mouth and eyebrows registering scorn, disgust and loathing in a manner which would have extorted the admiration of Patrolman Morehouse, himself no mean specialist in that direction.

'Sir?'

'I said viper.'

'Very good, sir. Your yoghurt, sir.'

'Take that stuff away.'

Joe and Kay came on to the terrace. They had been wandering through the rose garden, discussing ways and means. Kay's view was that love was all and that so long as they had each other, what did anything else matter? It was enough for her, she said, that she was going to marry Joe, because Joe was a woolly baa-lamb. Joe, while conceding that he was a woolly baa-lamb and admitting that love was swell, had rather tended to argue that a bit of the stuff would also come in handy, and from this the conversation turned naturally to Phipps, who in such a dastardly manner had placed that bit of stuff beyond their reach. It would be gratifying, said Joe, to have a word with Phipps. So, coming on to the terrace and seeing him there, he had it.

'Ha!' he said. 'Well, you sneaking, chiselling, two-timing, horn-swoggling highbinder!'

'Good morning, sir.'

Kay, too, was severe.

'I wonder you can look us in the face, Phipps.'

The butler sighed regretfully. His innate chivalry made the thought of having given offence to Youth and Beauty an unpleasant one.

'I am sorry to have been compelled to occasion you inconvenience, miss, but as Miss Shannon so well put it, it was military necessity. One cannot make an omelette without breaking eggs.'

He winced a little. Those overnight potations had left him in a condition where he would have preferred not to think of eggs. His breakfast that morning had consisted of a slice of Melba toast and three pots of black coffee, and even the Melba toast had seemed at the time excessive.

Joe had thought of another one.

'You wolf in butler's clothing!'

'Yes, sir. Precisely, sir,' said Phipps deferentially. He turned to Smedley. 'If you persist in refusing to drink your yoghurt, sir, I shall have no option but to inform Mrs Cork.'

Smedley endeavoured, as usual unsuccessfully, to snap his fingers.

'That for Mrs Cork!'

'Very good, sir.'

'You can go to Mrs Cork and tell her, with my compliments, to boil her head.'

'Very good, sir. I will bear your instructions in mind.'

The butler withdrew, to all appearances oblivious of the fact that six eyes were boring holes in his back, and the emotions of the three on the terrace found expression in words.

'The snake!' said Smedley.

'The hound!' said Joe.

'The reptile!' said Kay.

This made them all feel a little better, but only a little, for it was apparent to the dullest mind that what the crisis which had been precipitated called for was not words, but action. It was Smedley who clothed this thought in speech.

'We've got to do something,' said Smedley.

'But what?' said Joe.

'Yes, what?' said Kay.

There, Smedley admitted, they had him.

'Well, I'll tell you one thing,' he said. 'It's no good trying to formulate a plan of action without Bill. Where is Bill?'

'In the Garden Room,' said Kay. 'I saw her as we passed. I think she's working on Aunt Adela's *Memoirs*.'

'Then come on,' said Smedley.

Left to himself, he would rather not have revisited the Garden Room, with all its sad memories, but if Bill was there, to the Garden Room he must go. It was imperative that the conduct of affairs be handed over to The Old Reliable without delay. The thought crossed his mind that if Bill was capable of concentrating on Adela's ghastly *Memoirs* on the morning after a night like last night, she must be a woman of iron, and it encouraged him. There are certain difficult situations in life where a woman of iron at one's side is just what one most needs.

Bill, as fresh, so far as the eye could discern, as an infant newly risen from its afternoon nap, was seated at the desk, prattling away into the dictaphone as if without a care in the world.

'Ah, Hollywood, Hollywood,' said Bill. 'Bright city of sorrows, where fame deceives and temptation lurks, where souls are shrivelled in the furnace of desire and beauty is broken on sin's cruel wheel.' And if that was not the stuff to give them, she felt, she was vastly mistaken. There was a flat dullness about the story of Adela's life which made the injection of some such purple patch from time to time a necessity. Absolutely, as Lord Topham would have said.

Observing the procession filing in at the french window, she suspended her activities.

'Hello, boys and girls. Heavens, Smedley, you look like something left over from the Ark,' she said, and marvelled at the mysteries of a woman's heart, which can preserve its love for a man intact even when his appearance is that of flotsam and jetsam. For in describing Smedley as something left over from the Ark, she was really giving him the breaks. Actually, he resembled more closely one of those mildewed pieces of refuse found in dustbins, which are passed over with a disdainful jerk of the head by the discriminating alley cat.

Smedley exhibited pique. None knew better than he that he was not his usual spruce self and, like Regiomontanus, he felt that allowances ought to be made.

'How do you expect me to look?' he protested. 'I haven't been to bed for two nights. Bill, what are we going to do?'

'About Phipps?'

'Of course about Phipps. What else did you think we'd got on our minds?'

Bill nodded sympathetically.

'It's a problem,' she agreed. 'I ought to have reflected, before enlisting Phipps's services, that he is a man of infinite guile.'

'I'll sue him,' cried Smedley. 'I'll fight the case to the Supreme Court.'

'M'm.'

'Yes,' said Smedley, deflated, 'I suppose you're right. Then is there nothing we can do?'

'Can't you force him to give it up?' said Kay.

This pleased Smedley. The right spirit, he considered.

'Good idea. Intimidate the fellow. Stick lighted matches between his toes.'

Bill was obliged to discourage this Utopian dream.

'My dear Smedley, you can't stick lighted matches between the toes of an English butler. He would raise his eyebrows and freeze you with a glance. You'd feel as if he had caught you using the wrong fork. No, the only thing is to try an appeal to his better nature.' She rose, and pressed the bell. 'I guarantee no results. For all we know, Phipps hasn't a better nature.' She regarded Joe solicitously. 'You're looking very gloomy, Joe. Feeling a little low?'

'I could walk under a cockroach.'

'Cheer up. There is still joy in the world, still the happy laughter of children and the singing of bluebirds.'

'That's all right about bluebirds. I want to get married, and I'm down to my last ten dollars.'

Bill stared.

'Last ten dollars? What's become of that thousand you had?'

Joe's manner betrayed a certain embarrassment.

'Well, I'll tell you, Bill. You remember that gambling joint, Perelli's, we were talking about a couple of days ago? After the party broke up last night, I thought I'd go down there and try to make a fast buck.'

'Did you make a fast buck?'

'Unfortunately, no. But there's always a bright side. Perelli did.'

'He cleaned you out?'

'Except for ten dollars.'

'You unbalanced young boll weevil! Kay's right. You're not an *homme sérieux*.'

Kay flared up.

'He is not an unbalanced boll weevil. And what do you mean, saying he's not an *homme sérieux*? I think it was very sensible of him to go to Perelli's. It wasn't his fault he didn't win.'

Bill let it go. This, she felt, was love.

'And anyway, darling,' said Kay, 'I don't know what you are worrying about. Two can live as cheap as one.'

Bill regarded her admiringly.

'You do say some bright things, child. If that's your normal form, Joe won't have a dull moment in your little home.'

'In our little gutter, you mean,' corrected Joe.

'Joe says we shall have to starve in the gutter.'

'You can't,' said Bill. 'There aren't any gutters in Hollywood. Ah, come in, Phipps.'

The butler had manifested himself.

'You rang, madam?'

'Yes. Good morning, Phipps.'

'Good morning, madam.'

'Quite a night last night.'

'Yes, madam.'

'No ill effects, I trust?'

'I have a slight headache, madam.'

'Well earned. You should keep off the sauce, Phipps.'

'Yes, madam.'

'And now what about things?'

'On what particular point do you desire information, madam?'

Bill did not find his manner promising. Anything less resembling a butler likely to be talked with honeyed words into giving up a diary worth fifty thousand dollars she had never beheld. She persevered, however.

'About the diary. You remember it? It hasn't slipped your mind?'

'No, madam.'

'Having slept on the matter, you still propose to keep it?'

'Yes, madam.'

'And sell it and convert the proceeds to your own use?'

'Yes, madam.'

'Well, I don't want to hurt your feelings,' said Bill, 'but you must have a soul like a stevedore's undervest.'

The butler seemed rather pleased than otherwise. A faint twitch of the upper lip showed that if he had not been an English butler, he might have smiled.

'A very striking image, madam.'

'Has it occurred to you that you will have some exceedingly nasty questions to answer about this on Judgment Day?'

'No doubt, madam.'

'But you don't quail?'

'No, madam.'

Bill gave it up.

'All right, Phipps. You may withdraw.'

'Very good, madam.'

'What do you like at Santa Anita today?'

'Betty Hutton, madam, in the fourth race.'

'Thank you, Phipps.'

'Thank *you*, madam.'

CHAPTER 18

The door closed. Bill lit a cigarette.

'Well,' she said, 'I did my best. Nobody can do more. When you come up against Battling Phipps, you certainly know you've been in a fight.'

The door reopened.

'Excuse me, madam,' said Phipps. 'I inadvertently omitted to deliver a message entrusted to me by Mrs Cork. Mrs Cork presents her compliments and would be glad if Mr Smedley would join her in the projection room at his earliest convenience.'

Smedley did one of his quick dance steps.

'What? What does she want?'

'Mrs Cork did not honour me with her confidence, sir. But when I left her, she was standing scrutinizing the safe—'

'Oh, gosh!'

'– and heaving gently, sir, like a Welsh rarebit about to come to the height of its fever. Thank you, sir.'

The door closed again.

'Phipps has a very happy gift of phrase,' said Bill.

Smedley was plucking at his collar.

'Bill, she's found out.'

'She was bound to sooner or later.'

'She suspects me. What'll I do?'

'Stick to stout denial.'

'Stout denial?'

'Stout denial. You can't beat it. Get tough. Say "Oh, yeah?" and "Jussa minute, jussa minute", and when speaking, speak out of the side of the mouth.'

'Like Perelli,' said Joe.

'Does Mr Perelli speak out of the side of his mouth?'

'All the time.'

'Then there's your model, Smedley. Imagine that you're the proprietor of a prosperous gambling hell and that Adela is a dis-appointed client who is trying to sell you the idea that the wheel is crooked.'

Smedley went out, gulping unhappily. Bill wandered to the french window and looked out on the sunlit garden. Kay came to Joe, who after his brief observation about Mr Perelli had returned to the depths.

'Cheer up, darling,' she said. 'You still have me.'

'And ten dollars.'

'I call ten dollars quite a lot.'

'Yes, but when I leave here, I shall have to tip Phipps with it. Is that a bitter thought? If not,' said Joe, 'how would you describe it?' He looked at Bill, who was waving a friendly hand at some-one in the garden. 'What are you waving at?'

Bill turned.

'Come here, Joe.' She pointed. 'What do you see?'

Joe followed her finger with a dull eye.

'Clouds,' he said. 'Black, inky clouds. And murky shadows threatening doom, disaster and despair. Oh, you mean the figure in the foreground?'

'Right. My Lord Topham. He is coming this way, you observe.

How have you been getting along with Lord Topham since your arrival?'

'Pretty well. He was telling me about the trouble he has been having with a girl in England called Toots. Apparently she gave him the brusheroo, and he's a bit down about it.'

'You were sympathetic, I hope?'

'Oh, yes.'

'Good. Then he probably looks on you as a bosom friend. A very rich young man, Lord Topham, I understand,' said Bill meditatively. 'One of England's richest, Adela tells me. Something to do with chain stores or provision markets, if I am not mistaken. Anyway, however he gets the stuff, he's got it.'

Joe started. This opened up a new line of thought.

'Good Lord, Bill, you weren't thinking of touching Topham?'

'It is always a sound business principle, when you need twenty thousand dollars, to go to the man who's got twenty thousand dollars.'

'Bill, you're a genius.'

'That's what I kept telling those people at Superba-Llewellyn, but they wouldn't listen to me.'

'Pitch it strong, old friend.'

'I will, Joe, I will.'

The Lord Topham who a moment later dragged his long legs across the threshold of the french window and added his presence to the little group of thinkers in the Garden Room differed substantially from the exuberant young athlete who had made a similar entrance almost exactly twenty-four hours earlier. Then, it will be remembered, he had had a song on his lips and a gleam in his eye as the result of having broken a hundred on the golf links. For even an anxious lover, awaiting a reply to his well-expressed air mail letter from the girl with whom he has had a falling-out, will temporarily forget the sex angle after doing eighteen holes in ninety-seven strokes for the first time in his life. The Lord Topham of twenty-four hours ago, though the vultures of anxiety had presumably been gnawing at his vitals, had stood before the world as a definitely chirpy man.

Vastly different was the sombre figure that now loomed up behind its eleven-inch cigarette holder. The face was drawn, the eyes haggard, the general appearance that of one who has searched for the leak in life's gaspipe with a lighted candle. Even such a man, so faint, so spiritless, so dead, so dull in look, so woebegone, drew Priam's curtain in the dead of night and would have told him half his Troy was burned. One might have supposed, looking at him, that Lord Topham had been out on the links again and had not been able to do better than a hundred and fifty-seven, taking fourteen at the long dog-leg hole and losing six balls in the lake at the second.

Actually, what was causing his despondency was the fact that shortly after breakfast he had received the cable he had been expecting, and it had been a red-hot one. Miss Gladys ('Toots') Fauntleroy was one of those girls who do not object to letting the sun go down on their wrath, and it is to be doubted whether a more vitriolic ten-bobsworth had crossed the Atlantic Ocean since the days of the late Florenz Ziegfeld. It had caused hope to die and despair to take possession of Lord Topham's soul, and had engendered in him a comprehensive dislike for the whole human race. It was, in short, the worst possible moment anyone could have selected to approach him with the idea of getting into his ribs for twenty thousand dollars.

The newcomer's gloom did not impress itself on those present, so self-centred do we all tend to be in this world. Obsessed with their own personal problems, they merely saw a fabulously rich young man coming in through a french window. They did not pause to ask themselves if his heart was intact or broken, but clustered joyously about him, giving him a great reception.

'Lord Topham!' cried Kay. 'Do come in, Lord Topham.'

'Yes, do,' cried Joe. 'Just the man we wanted to see.'

'The very person,' said Bill. 'Lord Topham, old boy, could we have a word with you, Lord Topham, old boy?'

She patted his shoulder lovingly and another man in his position might have been pleased and touched by the warmth of her affection. He merely glowered down at her hand as if it had been one of those spiders for which Phipps had so strong a distaste.

'What the dickens are you doing?'

'Just patting your shoulder, Lord Topham, old boy, old boy.'

'Well, bally well don't,' said the old boy morosely.

A chill crept into the hearts of the reception committee. They looked at one another with a growing feeling of uneasiness. Something was wrong, they felt, something was seriously wrong. This was not the effervescent young man they had hoped to see. More like some sort of a changeling. It was with a feeling that little of a constructive nature was likely to result that Joe approached the main item on the agenda paper.

'Listen, Lord Topham. It is within your power to bring joy and happiness into quite a number of human lives.'

'Then I'm dashed if I'm going to do it,' said Lord Topham. 'Would it interest you to know how I feel about the human species? I hope it jolly well chokes. I don't mind telling you that I got a cable from my girl Toots this morning which has definitely turned me into a mis-what's-the-word. I mean one of those blokes who get fed up with their fellow men and go and live in caves and grow beards and subsist on berries from the bush and water from the spring. Don't talk to me about bringing joy into human lives. I have to do without joy, so why shouldn't the ruddy human lives? To blazes with them. Let 'em eat cake.'

'But if you don't help me, I'm ruined.'

'Well, that's fine,' said Lord Topham, brightening a little.

Phipps came softly in, and Bill regarded him with an unfriendly eye.

'You again?' she said. 'The way you keep shimmering in and out, one would think you were the family spectre.'

The butler preserved his equanimity.

'I came to inform his lordship that he was wanted on the telephone, madam. A transatlantic call, m'lord.'

Lord Topham quivered. The cigarette holder, which he had replaced between his lips at the conclusion of his powerful speech, fell to the ground, dashing its cigarette to fragments.

'Eh? What? A transatlantic call? Who is it?'

'A Miss Fauntleroy, m'lord.'

'What! Good Lord! Good heavens! Well, I'm dashed. Well, I'm blowed. Well, I'll be jiggered. Gangway, gangway, gangway!' cried Lord Topham, and was out of the room before one could have said 'What ho'. It seemed incredible that that elongated form, a moment ago so limp, could be capable of such speed on the flat.

Phipps, about to follow, was stopped by Bill.

'Oh, Phipps,' said Bill.

'Madam?'

'One moment, if I may delay your progress. Could you bring us some strengthening cocktails?'

'Certainly, madam.'

'Thank you, but don't go. When we were chatting just now, there was a point I omitted to touch on.'

'Yes, madam?'

'It is this. Had you a mother, Phipps?'

'Yes, madam.'

'Had she a knee?'

'Yes, madam.'

'Then did you not learn at that knee to do the square thing by all and sundry and not to go about steeping yourself in crime?'

'No, madam.'

'H'm. Negligence somewhere. All right, Phipps. Push off. Don't forget those cocktails.'

'I will put them in preparation immediately, madam.'

The door closed.

'Now what would Phipps's mother be like?' mused Bill. 'Something on the lines of Queen Victoria, I imagine.' She turned to Joe. 'Did you say "Oh, hell!"?'

'Yes.'

'I thought you did, and it wrung my heart. You take a dim view of the situation?'

'I do.'

'I don't. I have high hopes of Lord Topham.'

'What, after the way he was talking just now?'

'Forget the way he was talking just now. Since then his girl has called him on the transatlantic telephone. Girls don't dig down into their jeans for the price of a transatlantic telephone call unless love has re-awakened in their hearts, dispelling like the morning sun the mists of doubt and misunderstanding. I shall be greatly surprised if this does not mean that the second phase has set in – where the female love bird weeps on the male love bird's chest and says can he ever forgive her for speaking those cruel words.'

'Oh, Bill!' cried Kay.

'If such is the case, I don't think I am wrong in assuming that the milk of human kindness will have come surging back into the Topham bosom like a tidal wave, sweetening his outlook and rendering him a good and easy prospect.'

Joe nodded.

'Gosh, I believe you're right.'

'I feel sure of it. We shall see a very different Lord Topham in a moment or two.'

'And then you'll talk to him?'

'And then I'll talk to him.'

Footsteps sounded in the corridor, gay, galloping footsteps. The door was dashed open, and something that might have been a ray of sunshine in form-fitting grey flannel came curvetting over the threshold.

'I say,' cried this new and improved edition of Lord Topham. 'Everything's fine. Everything's all right. Everything's splendid.'

Bill patted his shoulder, this time without provoking a protest.

'Precisely what I was hoping when I heard that your heart throb was on the telephone. Get them calling up on the telephone, and it's in the bag. She loves you still?'

'Absolutely. She cried buckets, and I said: "There, there!" '

'You could hardly have put it more neatly.'

'She said she had a toothache when she sent that cable.'

'That soured her outlook?'

'Oh, definitely.'

'You mean absolutely, don't you?'

'That's right. Absolutely.'

'Well, well, well, I couldn't be more pleased. I'm delighted. We're all delighted. And now, Lord Topham, could you spare me a moment?'

'Oh, rather.'

'Fine.'

Bill led the young man to the sofa, deposited him there and took a seat at his side.

'Tell me, Lord Topham – or may I call you Topham?'

'Do. Or Toppy. Most of my pals call me Toppy.'

'What is your first name?'

'Lancelot. But I prefer to hush it up.'

'Then shall we settle for Toppy?'

'Absolutely.'

'Right. You notice I am patting your shoulder, again, Toppy. Would you like to know why?'

'Very much. I was just wondering.'

'I do it in a congratulatory spirit. Because I am going, Toppy, old boy, to let you in on a big thing.'

'Really?'

'Absolutely. Tell me, my dear Toppy, have you ever seen a man in a fur coat, with three chins, riding in a Rolls-Royce with a blonde on each knee and smoking a five-dollar cigar? Because, if so, you can be pretty sure he was a literary agent.'

'A what?'

'A literary agent.'

'What's that?'

'A literary agent – or authors' representative – is a man who sits in an arm-chair with his feet on a desk, full of caviare and champagne, and gives a couple of minutes to the authors who come crawling in on all fours, begging him to handle their out-put. Should he consent to do so, he takes ten per cent of the kitty.'

'What kitty would that be?'

'I refer to all emoluments received from these authors' works, which amount to very large sums indeed. Thus, we will suppose that this authors' representative sells a story by some client of his to a prominent editor for – well, taking a figure at random, forty thousand dollars. His cut would be four thousand.'

'It sounds like a jolly good show.'

'It is a jolly good show. Four thousand bucks for telling his secretary to shove a wad of typescript into an envelope and address, stamp and mail it is unquestionably nice sugar. And it's going on all the time.'

'All the time?'

'Practically without cessation. You would be astounded if you knew the amount of money that pours into the coffers of an authors' representative. New clients every hour of the day coming in and pleading to be allowed to give him ten per cent. Well, take an instance. He is sitting in his office one day after a lunch of nightingales' tongues washed down with Imperial Tokay, and in comes someone whom for want of a better name we will call Erle Stanley Gardner. He says: "Good afternoon, my dear authors' representative, would you as a favour to me agree to accept a tenth of my annual earnings? I should mention that I write sixteen books a year, and if only I can get out of the habit of eating, I think I could work it up to twenty. In short, counting in everything, serial, motion picture, radio, television and other rights, I should imagine that your take-home pay on me alone would be at least fifty or sixty thousand dollars per annum. Will you accept me as a client, my dear authors' representative?" And the authors' representative yawns and says he will try to fit him in. "Thank you, thank you," says Erle Stanley Gardner, and goes out. And scarcely has he left than in come Sinclair Lewis and Somerset Maugham. They say: "Good afternoon . . ." and – well, you get the idea. It's a bonanza.'

'A what?'

'A gold mine.'

'Oh, absolutely.'

'I knew you would see it, my dear Toppy. I knew I could rely on your swift intelligence. You have a mind like a razor. Now then, the point is that Joe here and I have the opportunity of buying an old established business of this nature.'

'An authors' representative business?'

'Just that.'

'You'll make a fortune.'

'Exactly. The same thought occurred to me. We shall have to spend the rest of our lives thinking up ways of doing down the income tax authorities. And all we need, to begin operations—'

'You'll have more money than you know what to do with.'

'We shall sprain our wrists, clipping coupons. And all we need—'

'So what I would suggest,' said Lord Topham, 'is that you slip me a hundred dollars as a temporary loan.'

Bill swayed a little.

'Eh?'

'You see,' said Lord Topham, 'owing to circumstances over which I have no control and which give me a headache whenever I try to understand them, I can't get a penny of my money out of England, not a solitary dashed penny. My pals tell me it's got something to do with there being a Labour Government, composed, as you doubtless know, of the most frightful cads and bounders. Well, this leaves me considerably strapped for the ready, so if you want to earn the undying gratitude of a bloke who is down to a cigarette case and a little small change, now's your chance.'

Bill looked up.

'Joe.'

'Yes?'

'Did you hear what I heard?'

'I did.'

'Then it wasn't just a ghastly dream.'

Lord Topham was going on to explain further.

'What put it into my mind to ask you was what you were saying about your extraordinary wealth. Here, on the one hand, I said to myself, is this dear, sweet creature rolling in the stuff, and here, on the other hand, am I, unable to raise a bean on account of the sinister goings-on of this bally Labour Government who go about seeking whom they may devour. So pretty naturally the thought floated into my mind "Well, dash it!" I mean, a hundred dollars means nothing to you . . .'

A weary look came into Bill's rugged face.

'Have you a hundred dollars, Joe? No, I remember you haven't. Then I suppose . . . Here you are, Toppy.'

'Thanks,' said Lord Topham. 'Thanks most awfully. Yo ho! You know what this means? It means that I can now go to Santa Anita this afternoon with a light heart, ready for any fate. Phipps tells me Betty Hutton is a snip for the fourth and . . . Well, in a nutshell, my dear good preserver, thanks awfully. May heaven bless you, my jolly old multi-millionairess. Yo ho!' said Lord Topham. 'Yo frightfully absolutely ho!'

He passed through the french window on winged feet.

CHAPTER 19

Bill drew a deep breath. Her face was careworn, as if hers was the head upon which all the sorrows of the world had come, and when at length she found speech, she spoke dully.

'So that's that,' she said. 'A disappointment, Joe.'

'Quite.'

'Upsetting.'

'Most.'

'Yes, distinctly upsetting. Until that last awful moment everything seemed to be going so well. It makes me feel as if I had been chasing rainbows and one of them had turned and bitten me in the leg. If only I had remembered to give a thought to existing financial conditions in the British Isles, I would have been spared a painful experience. My last hundred dollars – gone – just like that. And for what? To enable a goofy English peer to back his fancy on the Santa Anita racecourse. Oh, well, I suppose it all tends to make one more spiritual. Ah, Smedley,' she said, as the door opened. 'What news from the throbbing centre of things?'

Smedley was looking warm and glassy-eyed, like a sensitive director of a shaky limited liability company emerging from a stormy meeting of shareholders. It was plain that whatever had passed between him and his sister-in-law in the projection room had not been in the nature of a love feast.

'She's as mad as a wet hen,' he said.

'Too bad,' said Bill. 'One hates to cause Adela distress. What happened?'

'She swears we've got the thing.'

'She little knows. Did you try stout denial?'

'Yes, but it didn't do any good. You can't drive an idea out of Adela's head, once it's in it. You know what she's like.'

'I do, indeed.'

Smedley mopped his forehead. There was a suggestion in his deportment of Shadrach, Meshach and Abednego coming out of the burning fiery furnace.

'Gosh, I'm a nervous wreck. I wish I had a drink.'

'Phipps will be bringing cocktails in a moment. Ah,' said Bill. 'Here, if I mistake not, is our client now.'

Phipps entered, bearing a loaded tray that tinkled musically. He laid it on the desk with his usual air of being a plenipotentiary to some great court delivering important documents.

'So what was the upshot?' said Bill.

'Eh?' said Smedley, who had been eyeing the cocktails.

'How did it all come out in the end?'

'Adela? Oh, she stuck to it that we had opened the safe, and she seemed to think you were the one who had got the diary. She put on a big act, and finished by saying she had phoned for the police.'

'What?'

A sudden light came into Bill's eye. Her despondency had left her. She was once more The Old Reliable in full command of the situation.

'The police are coming here? Then I think I see daylight. It's better than the arrival of the United States Marines. Phipps!'

'Madam?'

'I greatly fear, Phipps, that you are in a spot. Did you hear what Mr Smedley said?'

'No, madam. My attention was occupied with depositing the cocktails, madam.'

Bill gave him a sympathetic look.

'Stick close to those cocktails, Brother Phipps. You'll be needing one in just a moment. Mr Smedley said that Mrs Cork has sent for the cops.'

'Indeed, madam?'

'I admire your icy coolness. In your place I would be trembling like a leaf.'

'I do not follow your drift, madam.'

'I will continue snowing. The officers of the Law are on their way here, and what will they do when they get here, these officers of the Law? They will spread a dragnet. They will case the joint. They will go through the place with a fine-tooth comb.'

'So I imagine, madam.'

'They will find your hiding place, the secret nook where you have cached that diary. And then what?'

The butler remained politely puzzled.

'Are you hinting that they might suspect me of the robbery, madam?'

Bill laughed raspingly.

'Well, considering that you have an established place in the hall of fame as an expert safeblower, whom else would they suspect? It begins to look like a sticky weekend for you, Phipps.'

'I disagree with you, madam. It is true that the constables will probably discover the object under advisement, but I have merely to explain that in abstracting it I was operating on Mr Smedley's behalf. My position was that of an agent acting for a principal.'

Bill raised her eyebrows.

'I don't understand you. Are you suggesting that you were *asked* to open the safe? You don't know anything about this, do you, Smedley?'

'Not a thing.'

'You never asked Phipps to open the safe?'

'Certainly not.'

'Did you, Joe?'

'No.'

'Kay?'

'No.'

'Nor did I. The trouble with you, Phipps, is that you will insist on trying to hide your light beneath a bushel. Quite independently and on your own you conceive this brilliant idea of busting the safe and pinching its contents, and you try to give the credit to others. It shows a generous spirit which one cannot help but admire, and in recognition of our admiration we should like to do something for you. Hand the thing over to Mr Smedley, and he will take charge of it. Then you won't have anything to worry about. You follow my reasoning?'

'Yes, madam.'

'I thought you would. Go and get it.'

'I have it on my person, madam.'

Without any visible emotion the butler drew the book from his pocket, placed it on a salver and brought it to Smedley, who took it like a trout jumping at a fly.

'Would there be anything further, madam?'

'No, thank you, Phipps. You will receive your agent's commission, of course.'

Smedley started.

'What, after this?'

'Certainly. We must keep the books straight. And we agents stick together. You will receive your cut in due course, Phipps.'

'Thank you, madam.'

'Sorry you have been troubled.'

'Not at all, madam.'

'After all, you have your Art.'

'Precisely, madam,' said Phipps, and made a decorous withdrawal.

Joe was eyeing Bill devoutly, like a man gazing at some great public monument. His feelings were for a moment too deep for utterance, but eventually he managed to tell Bill she was a marvel.

'She certainly is,' said Kay.

'She ought to have that brain of hers pickled and presented to some national museum,' said Smedley, equally enthusiastic.

'When she's done with it.'

'When she's done with it, of course,' assented Smedley. 'Well, I'm off to see that gardener at the Lulabelle Mahaffys, to get him to translate this thing for me. I shall be in a stronger position to bargain with those fellows at Colossal-Exquisite if I know what's in it.'

'You are going to close with Colossal-Exquisite's offer?' said Bill.

'If it's still firm. Fifty thousand dollars is a nice round sum.'

Bill agreed.

'Very nice. Very round. Yes, I'd take it. Get their cheque, lay aside five thousand for Phipps, slip Joe and me our twenty thousand, and you'll be set.'

Smedley, who had been making for the french window, briskly like a man to whom time is money, paused. He seemed perplexed.

'Joe and you? Twenty thousand? I don't get this. What are you talking about?'

'For the literary agency.'

'What literary agency?'

'You told me you would put up the money for it,' said Joe.

Smedley stared.

'I said I would put up money for a literary agency? When?'

'The night before last. When we were at Mocambo.'

'This is the first I have heard of this.'

'What! But we were talking about it for hours. Don't you remember?'

Bill was looking grave.

'I was afraid this might happen, Joe. Smedley has a memory like a sieve.'

Smedley bridled.

'I have an excellent memory,' he said stiffly. 'But I certainly have not the slightest recollection of ever having heard a literary agency mentioned. What is this literary agency?'

'The one Bill and I want to buy.'

'And you construed some passing remark of mine into a promise that I would lend you the money?'

'Passing remark be damned. We discussed it for about an hour and a half. You kept patting me on the back and telling me over and over again—'

Smedley shook his head.

'Some mistake. The thing's absurd on the face of it. I wouldn't put up money for a literary agency. Much too risky. I'm going to go back to New York and get into the producing game again. I shall take an office and let it be known that I am prepared to consider scripts. Bless my soul, it will be quite like old times. Well, I can't stand here talking,' said Smedley. 'See you all later.'

He went out, and Joe and Kay, after an instant's stunned silence, came to life and bounded after him. Their voices died away across the garden, and Bill sat down at the dictaphone.

'Ah, Hollywood, Hollywood,' said Bill. 'Home of mean glories and spangled wretchedness, where the deathless fire burns for the outspread wings of the guileless moth, whose streets are bathed in the shamed tears of betrayed maidens.'

She looked up as the door opened.

'Ah, Adela,' she said welcomingly. 'I thought you might be looking in. Yo ho! Yo frightfully absolutely ho!'

Adela was looking even more formidable than usual, and her voice when, after fixing Bill for some moments with a baleful stare, she finally spoke, vibrated with stormy emotion.

'So there you are, Wilhelmina.'

It took more than a vibrating voice to lower Bill's morale. She nodded with what seemed to her sister insufferable heartiness.

'Yes, here I am, working away as always. I was just recording your views on Hollywood at the time when Bioscope wouldn't give you a job.'

Adela continued to stare balefully.

'Never mind my views on Hollywood. Wilhelmina, I would like a word with you.'

'A thousand.'

'Five will do. Wilhelmina, where is that diary?'

Bill wrinkled her forehead.

'Diary? Diary?' Her face cleared. 'Oh, you mean the one you were taking care of for Smedley? Isn't it in your safe?'

'You know very well it is not in my safe.'

'I thought you put it there.'

'I did, and it is there no longer. I will give you two minutes to produce it.'

'Me?'

'After that I wash my hands of the matter and the Law can take its course.'

Bill held up a hand.

'Wait. It's coming back. Yes, I thought that line was familiar. It was a sub-title in your *Gilded Sinners*. Do you remember? Where you came in and found your sister burgling the safe?'

'As happened last night.'

'I don't understand you.'

Her pent-up feelings were too much for Adela. She picked up a cocktail glass and flung it emotionally against the opposite wall.

'Sweet artichokes of Jerusalem!' she cried. 'Do you want it in words of one syllable? Then you shall have it. You – stole – that – diary.'

'Diary is three syllables.'

There was a pause. Bill, too, picked up a cocktail glass, but with the intention of making a better use of it than her sister had done. She rattled the shaker with pleasurable anticipation. No other sound broke the silence. Adela was clenching and unclenching her fists, and her eyes were stony. Her late husband, Alfred Cork, encountering her in this mood one morning after he had been out all night playing poker, had taken one look at her and left for Mexico City without stopping to pack. On Bill her demeanour seemed to have made a less pronounced impression. She filled her glass, and drank its amber contents with a satisfied sigh.

'Well?' said Adela. 'Are you going to have the effrontery to deny it?'

Bill seemed amused. She refilled her glass, paying a silent tribute to the absent Phipps. Jimmy Phipps might be about as slippery a customer as ever breathed the pure air of Beverly

Hills, with a moral code which would have caused comment in Alcatraz, but he knew how to mix cocktails.

'But, my dear Adela, I can't open safes.'

'You have friends who can. Your friends are well known to be the scum of the earth, thugs who would stick at nothing.'

'The only friend of mine on the premises last night was Joe Davenport, and you can hardly suspect Joe of being a safeblower. Why, you might just as well suspect Phipps. No,' said Bill, sipping the butler's masterpiece reverently. 'An outside job, if you ask me.'

'An outside job!'

'That's right. Probably the work of an international gang. Damn' clever, these international gangs. Have a cocktail?'

'I will not have a cocktail.'

'You're missing something good. Unlike the international gang.'

Bill's respect for Phipps deepened. The man seemed to have everything. Not only could he mix the perfect martini, but as a word-painter he stood second to none. He had described Adela as looking like a Welsh rarebit about to come to the height of its fever, and it was such a Welsh rarebit at the critical stage of its preparation that she now resembled. In times of crisis, Smedley was a great shaker in every limb, but he would have had to yield first place to Adela Shannon Cork.

'So you wish me to believe,' said Adela, having struggled with her feelings, 'that it was just a coincidence that my safe was burgled on the one night when it contained that diary?'

'A pure coincidence.'

'A pretty coincidence.'

'And I'm afraid, a most unfortunate coincidence – for you.'

Adela stared.

'What do you mean?'

Bill shrugged her shoulders.

'Surely it's obvious?'

'Not to me.'

Bill's manner became grave. There was concern in it, and sympathy. She hesitated a moment, as if reluctant to break the bad news. One could see she was sorry for Adela.

'Well, consider your position,' she said. 'Smedley had a firm offer of fifty thousand dollars for that diary. He wanted to keep it on his person, but you officiously insisted on taking it from him and putting it in your safe. In other words, you voluntarily assumed full responsibility for it.'

'Nonsense.'

'You won't find it nonsense when Smedley brings a suit against you for fifty thousand dollars.'

'What?'

'Don't forget that he has three witnesses to testify that you took the thing against his expressed wishes. There isn't a jury in America that won't give him your head on a charger.'

'Nonsense.'

'Keep on saying "Nonsense", if it comforts you. I'm merely stating the cold facts. Fifty thousand dollars is what that intelligent jury will award to Smedley, without so much as leaving the jury box. Fortunately you're a millionairess, so it doesn't matter to you. Unless you're one of those women who don't like having to pay out fifty thousand dollars. Some women don't.'

Adela groped her way to the sofa and collapsed on it.

'But – but—'

'I told you you ought to have a cocktail.'

'But this is absurd.'

'Not absurd. Disastrous. I can't see how the cleverest lawyer could make out any case for you. Smedley will win hands down.'

Adela had taken out her handkerchief and was twisting it agitatedly. Much, if not all, of her stormy emotion had been drained from her. When she spoke, there was quite a fluttering note in her voice.

'But, Wilhelmina—'

'Yes, Adela?'

'But, Wilhelmina, can't you reason with Smedley?'

Bill finished her cocktail and sighed contentedly.

'Now we're getting down to it,' she said with satisfaction. 'Now we're arriving somewhere. I *have* reasoned with Smedley.'

'You have?'

'Yes, he was in here just now, breathing fire and fury. I never saw a man so worked up. Adamant, he was. Insisted on the full amount and not a cent less. You should have seen him striding about the room like a tiger. I doubted at first if I would be able to do anything with him. But I kept after him. I pointed out what a nuisance these lawsuits were and urged him to agree to a settlement. And in the end, you'll be glad to hear, I beat him down to thirty thousand.'

'Thirty thousand!'

'I knew you'd be pleased,' said Bill. She looked at her sister incredulously. 'Do you mean you *aren't* pleased?'

Adela choked.

'It's highway robbery.'

Bill could not follow her.

'I would call it a perfectly ordinary business transaction. Owing to you, Smedley is down fifty thousand dollars. He very decently agrees to accept thirty. Pretty square of him, I should have said. Still, have it your own way. Let him bring his suit, if that's the way you want it. If you would rather pay fifty thousand than thirty thousand, that's your affair. Eccentric, though, it seems to me.'

'But, Wilhelmina—'

Bill pointed out another aspect of the matter.

'Of course, it will mean a lot of unpleasant publicity, I'm afraid. You won't show up well at the trial, you know. The impression the public will get from the evidence is that you're the sort of woman who is not to be trusted alone with anything that isn't nailed down. When your friends see you coming, they will hurriedly store their little valuables in a stout chest and sit on the lid till you are out of sight. Louella Parsons is hardly likely to refrain from comment on the affair, nor is Hedda Hopper. And I should imagine that the *Hollywood Reporter* would consider you front-page stuff. But as I say,' said Bill, 'have it your own way.'

The picture she had conjured up decided Adela. She rose.

'Oh, very well.' She paused for a moment, to overcome a sudden urge to scream and break the remaining cocktail glasses. 'It's an outrage, but ... Oh, very well.'

Bill nodded approvingly. One likes to see one's flesh and blood reasonable.

'Good,' she said. 'I'm glad you're taking the sensible view. Trot along to your boudoir and write the cheque. Make it out to me. Smedley has appointed me his agent, to handle the affair.' She accompanied Adela to the door. 'Gosh, how relieved you must be feeling,' she said. 'You would probably like to go into a buck and wing dance.'

Phipps appeared.

'The constables are here, madam.'

'Oh, damn the constables,' said Adela, and sailed past him.

Bill gave the butler a grave look.

'You must excuse Mrs Cork, Phipps, if she is a little brusque. She has just had a bereavement.'

'I am sorry, madam.'

'I, too. Still, these things are sent to us for a purpose. Maybe to make us more spiritual.'

'Quite possibly, madam.'

'You're looking a bit spiritual yourself, Phipps.'

'Thank you, madam.'

'Not at all. Show the officers in.'

'Very good, madam.'

Joe and Kay came through the french window. They were looking dejected.

'Well?' said Bill.

'No luck,' said Joe.

'He wouldn't listen,' said Kay.

This caused Bill no surprise.

'Smedley is a bad listener. He reminds me of the deaf adder with whom the charmers had so much trouble. But cheer up, Joe. All is well.'

Joe stared.

'All is *what*?'

'Everything's fine.'

'Who says so?'

'I say so.'

'The constables, madam,' announced Phipps.

Sergeant Ward entered, followed by Patrolman Morehouse. Bill greeted them effusively.

'Well, well, well,' she said. 'How delightful seeing you again.'

'Good morning, ma'am.'

'I was thinking only just now how nice it would be if you were to drop in once more. Too often in this world we meet a strange face and say to ourselves: "Have I found a friend? I believe I have found a friend. Yes, by golly, I'm *sure* I've found a friend", and then – *bing* – the face pops off and you never see it again.' She peered at them. 'But you're looking extraordinarily cheerful,' she said. 'Has some good fortune come your way?'

The sergeant beamed. The patrolman beamed.

'I'll say it has,' said the patrolman. 'Tell her, sarge.'

'Well, ma'am,' said the sergeant, his granite face wreathed in smiles, 'we've done it.'

'You don't mean—?'

'Yes, ma'am. Got a call this morning from the Medulla-Oblongata-Glutz casting office. We start tomorrow.'

'Well, well. Joy cometh in the morning.'

'Yes, ma'am. Of course, it's only extra work.'

'Only extra work right now,' said Patrolman Morehouse.

'Sure,' said Sergeant Ward. 'Just for the moment. We expect to rise in our profession.'

'Of course you'll rise,' said Bill. 'Like rockets. First, extra work, then bit parts, then big parts, then bigger parts, and finally stardom.'

'Ah!' said the sergeant. 'Hot dog!'

'Hot dog,' said the patrolman.

'You'll be bigger than Gary Cooper.'

'Hell, yes,' said the sergeant. 'What's Gary Cooper ever done?'

Adela came in. She had a slip of paper in her hand, but there was nothing in her demeanour to indicate that she enjoyed carrying it. She came to Bill and gave it to her, reluctantly like a woman parting with life blood.

'There,' she said.

'Thank you, Adela.'

'And may I remark that I wish you had been strangled at birth.'

The sergeant saluted.

'You sent for us, ma'am?'

'Yes,' said Bill, 'but it was a mistake. My sister thought her safe had been robbed last night. It wasn't.'

'Ah? Well, that's how it goes,' said the sergeant.

'That's how it goes,' said the patrolman.

'Good morning,' said Adela.

'Good morning, ma'am,' said the sergeant.

'Hey!' said the patrolman. 'Excuse me, lady, but may I have your autograph, ma'am?'

Adela paused at the door. She swallowed once or twice before speaking.

'You may not,' she said. 'And one more word out of you on the subject of autographs – or any other subject – and I'll pull your fat head off and make you swallow it. Good MORNING.'

The door slammed. The sergeant looked at the patrolman. The patrolman looked at the sergeant.

'Women!' said the sergeant.

'Women!' said the patrolman.

'Can you beat them!' said the sergeant.

'Why, yes,' said Bill. 'Sometimes. But you need to be a woman yourself and very, very clever – like me. Here, Joe,' she said, and handed him the cheque.

He looked at it listlessly, then staggered.

'Bill! Good heavens, Bill!'

Bill patted her chest.

'The Old Reliable!' she said. 'Which way did Smedley go? I want a word with him.'

The home of the Lulabelle Mahaffys, whose gardens were tended by the Mexican gentleman with whom Smedley had gone to confer, stood some two hundred yards down the road from the Carmen Flores place, and it did not take Bill long to cover the distance. She had just arrived in sight of the gate, when she saw Smedley come out and start walking toward her. He was whistling, and there was a jauntiness in his step which bespoke the soul at rest.

'Well?' she said. 'Did you see him?'

'Oh, hello, Bill,' said Smedley. 'No, he wasn't there. It's his day off. But it doesn't matter. I was just coming back to ask you to lend me that jalopy of yours. I want to go down and see those people at Colossal-Exquisite. Bless my soul,' said Smedley, casting an approving glance at the blue sky, 'what a glorious day.'

'For you.'

Smedley was not a man of quick perceptions, but even he could appreciate that this morning, which had brought such happiness to him, had been more sparing with the ecstasy as regarded others. He recalled now, what he had neglected to observe at the time of their meeting, that both his niece Kay and that young fellow Davenport had exhibited not a few signs of distress of mind when chatting with him.

'What was all that nonsense young Davenport was talking about a literary agency?' he asked. 'He seemed very excited about it, but I was too busy to listen.'

'Joe and I were thinking of buying one.'

'You? Are you in it too?'

'That's right. As was carefully explained to you. You're like a Wednesday matinée audience, Smedley. You miss the finer points.'

Smedley puffed – remorsefully, it seemed.

'Well, I'm sorry, Bill.'

'Don't give it a thought.'

'But you can understand how I'm placed, a sensible woman like you. I can't afford to go putting up money for literary agencies.'

'You prefer something safer and more conservative, like backing shows on Broadway?'

'That's where the big money is,' said Smedley defensively. 'How much do you think someone would have made if they'd bought in on *Oklahoma*?'

'Or *South Pacific*.'

'Or *Arsenic And Old Lace*.'

'Or *Ladies, I Beg You*,' said Bill, mentioning the little stinker adapted from the French which had cost the other the last thousands of his waning capital.

Smedley blushed. He did not like to be reminded of *Ladies, I Beg You*.

'That was just an unfortunate accident.'

'So that's what you call it?'

'It can't happen again. I shall be bringing to the business now a wealth of experience and a ripened judgment.'

'Ripened judgment, did you say?'

'Ripened judgment.'

'I see. Ripened judgment. God bless you, Smedley,' said Bill, giving him the tender look a mother gives her idiot child. She was feeling, not for the first time, that it was criminal to allow her old friend to run around loose, without a woman's hand to guide him. Somewhere in America, she told herself, there might be a more pronounced fathead than this man she had loved so long, but it would be a weary search, trying to find him.

A klaxon tooted in their rear. If it is possible for a tooter to toot respectfully and deferentially, this tooter did. They turned, and saw approaching a natty little roadster, at whose wheel sat Phipps. It is a very impoverished butler in Beverly Hills who does not own his natty little roadster.

He drew up beside them, and Bill noted suitcases on the seat. It seemed that Phipps was flitting.

'Hello, my bright and bounding Phipps,' she said. 'You off?'

'Yes, madam.'

'Leaving us for good?'

'Yes, madam.'

'Rather sudden?'

'Yes, madam. Strictly speaking my tenure of office should not have expired until the day after tomorrow, but I chanced to encounter Mrs Cork not long since, and she expressed a wish that I should curtail my stay.'

'She told you to get out?'

'That was substantially the purport of her words, madam. Mrs Cork seemed somewhat stirred.'

'I told you she had had a bereavement.'

'Yes, madam.'

'So this – is goodbye?'

'Yes, madam.'

Bill dabbed at her eyes.

'Well, it's been nice seeing you.'

'Thank you, madam.'

'I'll say this for you, Brother Phipps, that when you're around, there's never a dull moment. We part with no hard feelings, I trust?'

'Madam?'

'About that diary.'

'Oh, no, madam. None whatever.'

'I'm glad you can take the big, broad view.'

'I find it easier to do so, madam, because the brochure which I handed to Mr Smedley at the conclusion of our recent conversation was not the diary of the late Miss Flores.'

Smedley, who had been gazing stiffly into the middle distance, as if resolved not to show himself aware of the presence of one whom he considered, and always would consider, a viper of the first water, suddenly ceased to be aloof and detached. He transferred his gaze to the butler, and his eyes popped, as was their custom when he was deeply moved.

'What? '

'No, sir.'

'What are you talking about?'

'It was a little thing I borrowed from the cook, sir.'

'But it's in Spanish.'

'I think you will find that it is not, sir, if you will examine it, sir.'

Smedley whipped the volume from his pocket, gave it a quick glance and registered triumph.

'Spanish!'

'You are mistaken, sir.'

'Damn it, man, look for yourself.'

Phipps took the book in his deferential way.

'Yes, sir, I was wrong.' He put the book in his pocket. 'You are quite right, sir. Spanish. Good day, sir. Good day, madam.'

He placed a shapely foot on the accelerator.

'Hey!' cried Smedley.

But there was no answer. Phipps had said his say. The car gathered speed. It turned the corner, beyond which lay the broad road leading to Beverly Hills. Like some lovely dream that vanishes at daybreak, James Phipps had gone out of their lives.

That Smedley was reluctant to see him go was manifest in his whole bearing. He did not actually say 'Oh, for the touch of a vanished hand!' but the words were implicit in his actions. Breaking into a clumsy gallop, he started in pursuit. But these natty roadsters are hard to catch, particularly if you are a man of elderly middle age and sedentary habits. If Smedley had been capable of doing the quarter-mile in forty-nine seconds, he might have accomplished something to his advantage, but his distance was the ten-yard dash, and he was not very good even at that.

Presently he came back to Bill, panting and passing a handkerchief over a streaming brow, and Bill stared at him with honest amazement.

'If I hadn't seen it with my own eyes,' said Bill, 'I wouldn't have believed it. You gave it to him. You handed it to him. If you had served it up to him on an individual skewer smothered in onions, you couldn't have done more.'

Smedley writhed beneath her scorn.

'Well, how could I know he was going to—'

'Of course you couldn't,' said Bill. 'After having exactly the same thing happen yesterday with Adela, how could the thought have entered your mind? And what possible reason could you have to suspect a man like Phipps of anything in the least resembling raw work? All your dealings with him must have established him in your mind as a stainless soul and a paragon of spotless rectitude. Honestly, Smedley, you ought to be in some sort of home.'

'Well, I—'

'Or married,' said Bill.

Smedley quivered as if the two simple words had been a couple of harpoons plunged into his shrinking flesh. He shot an apprehensive look at Bill, and did not like the determined expression on her rugged face.

'Yes,' she said, 'that's what you need – marriage. You want someone to look after you and shield you from the world, and by the greatest good luck I know the very woman to do it. Smedley, I have been potty about you for twenty years – heaven knows why—'

'Bill, please!'

'And, if you didn't suspect it, what probably misled you was the fact that I never told my love, but let concealment like a worm i' the bud feed on my damask cheek. I pined in thought, and with a green and yellow melancholy—'

'No, Bill, really!'

'– sat like Patience on a monument, smiling at grief. But now I have changed my act, and, like Adela, I intend to stand no nonsense. I cannot offer you luxury, Smedley. All I have to lay at your feet is a literary agency which Adela is backing to the tune of thirty thousand dollars.'

Smedley had not supposed that anything would have had the power to divert his mind from the hideous vision of matrimony which her words had brought before his eyes, but this did.

'Adela?' he gasped. 'She's given you thirty thousand dollars?'

'With a merry smile and a jolly pat on the back. And tomorrow Joe and I start for New York and get our noses down to the grindstone. It will be hard work, of course, and it would be nice to have you at our side, doing your bit. For I am convinced that in a literary agency you would find your niche, Smedley. You have the presence which would impress authors. I can just see you giving them five minutes. Editors, too. That Roman Emperor deportment of yours would lay editors out cold. But I can see why you hesitate. You are reluctant to give up your life of luxury under Adela's roof, with yoghurt flowing like water and Adela always on hand for a stimulating chat ... By the way, I wonder how you stand with Adela just now. She may be the least bit sore with you after all that has occurred, and when Adela is sore with anyone, she shows it in her manner.'

Smedley paled.

'Oh, gosh!'

'Yes, you may not find those chats with her so stimulating, after all. You'd better marry me, Smedley.'

'But, Bill—'

'I am only speaking for your own good.'

'But, Bill ... Marriage ...'

'What's wrong with marriage? It's fine. Why, look at the men who liked it so much that, once started, they couldn't stop, and just went on marrying everything in sight. Look at Brigham Young. Look at Henry the Eighth. Look at King Solomon. Those boys knew when they were on a good thing.'

Out of the night that covered him, black as the pit from pole to pole, there shone on Smedley a faint glimmer of light. Something like hope dawned in him. He weighed what she had just said.

Brigham Young – Henry the Eighth – King Solomon – knowledgeable fellows, all of them, men whose judgment you could trust. And they had liked being married, so much so that, as Bill had indicated, they made a regular hobby of it. Might it not quite easily prove, mused Smedley, that marriage was not, as it was generally called, the fate that is worse than death, but something that has its points?

Bill saw his drawn face light up. She linked her arm in his and gave it a squeeze.

'Wilt thou, Smedley,' she said, 'take this Wilhelmina?'

'I will,' said Smedley in a low but firm voice.

Bill kissed him tenderly.

'That's my little man,' she said. 'This afternoon we'll go out in my jalopy and start pricing ministers.'

THE END

Aunts Aren't Gentlemen
Barmy in Wonderland
Big Money
Bill the Conqueror
Blandings Castle
Carry On, Jeeves
The Clicking of Cuthbert
Cocktail Time
The Code of the Woosters
The Coming of Bill
A Damsel in Distress
Do Butlers Burgle Banks?
Doctor Sally
Eggs, Beans and Crumpets
A Few Quick Ones
Frozen Assets
Full Moon
Galahad at Blandings
A Gentleman of Leisure
The Girl in Blue
The Girl on the Boat
The Gold Bat
The Heart of a Goof
Heavy Weather
Hot Water
Ice in the Bedroom
Indiscretions of Archie
The Inimitable Jeeves
Jeeves and the Feudal Spirit
Jeeves in the Offing
Jill the Reckless
Joy in the Morning
Laughing Gas
Leave it to Psmith
The Little Nugget
Lord Emsworth and Others
Love Among the Chickens
The Luck of the Bodkins

The Man Upstairs
The Man with Two Left Feet
The Mating Season
Meet Mr Mulliner
Money for Nothing
Money in the Bank
Mr Mulliner Speaking
Much Obliged, Jeeves
Mulliner Nights
My Man Jeeves
Nothing Serious
The Old Reliable
A Pelican at Blandings
Piccadilly Jim
Pigs Have Wings
Plum Pie
The Pothunters
A Prefect's Uncle
Psmith in the City
Psmith, Journalist
Quick Service
Right Ho, Jeeves
Ring for Jeeves
Sam the Sudden
Service with a Smile
Something Fishy
Something Fresh
Spring Fever
Stiff Upper Lip, Jeeves
Summer Lightning
Summer Moonshine
Thank You, Jeeves
Ukridge
Uncle Dynamite
Uncle Fred in the Springtime
Uneasy Money
Very Good, Jeeves!
Young Men in Spats

This edition of P. G. Wodehouse has been prepared from the first British printing of each title.

The Everyman Wodehouse is printed on acid-free paper and set in Caslon, a typeface designed and engraved by William Caslon of William Caslon & Son, Letter-Founders in London around 1740.